Gray

A SHADOW OPS TEAM NOVEL

D1519429

Makenna Jameison

Copyright © 2024 by Makenna Jameison

ISBN: 9798340374653

ALSO BY MAKENNA JAMEISON

SHADOW OPS TEAM

Jett
Ford
Luke
Sam
Mistletoe Mischief
Nick
Gray

Table of Contents

Prologue

One month ago

Lena mumbled, trying to get her bearings as the world shifted around her. She was tired. So damn tired. Her entire body felt heavy and too weak to move, like she couldn't get up even if she tried. Even her thoughts were sluggish. Confused.

Was she in bed?

No. Because it felt like she was moving. Swaying.

Her eyelids wouldn't open, her body too exhausted to do anything she wanted, but she could sense it was daytime. Warm sunlight caressed her skin.

It almost felt like she was floating now. She was warm and so, so sleepy.

As she began to drift off again, low voices made her realize she wasn't alone.

Wait. Was she riding in a car? A memory niggled at the back of her mind, just out of reach. She was supposed to do something. Be somewhere. She'd been with friends earlier, she realized. They'd had coffee. Gone back inside. Suddenly, her stomach dropped.

"Kaylee!" she cried out, her voice hoarse.

"Shhh." A rough hand gently smoothed her hair back from her face, and relief coursed through her at the sound of the gruff voice. His touch felt so gentle against her skin. So damn careful.

Safe.

She was safe.

And she knew the man holding her would die rather than let those evil men hurt her.

"We're almost to the hospital," another male voice said. "Five more minutes."

Lena stiffened again, but then the soothing voice was calming her once more, drowning out her panic. "Lena, we're almost there. Stay with me, baby. Try to stay awake."

"Gray?" she murmured.

"That's right. It's Gray. You were drugged," he continued, and she realized Gray wasn't just beside her in the car, he was holding her in his strong arms, her head resting on his shoulder. "Your pulse is weak. We're taking you to the emergency room. Everything will be okay now."

Suddenly, relief washed over her. She wasn't in the dark SUV with the armed men who'd tracked down Kaylee. She wasn't in the house they'd taken her to— in the bedroom of the man who was meaner, harder than all the others.

Lena opened her mouth, a million questions churning in her mind, but no words came out. Had hours passed since she and Kaylee had been kidnapped? Days? Why couldn't she remember

8

exactly what had happened?

Had she been assaulted in that house?

Lena whimpered.

"Shhh." Gray's big hand stroked the back of her head, comforting her. "Luke is driving us to the hospital. Kaylee's okay, too. You're going to be fine. You were unconscious when we found you, sweetheart."

Lena must've passed out again, because the next thing she knew, someone was carrying her toward the emergency room entrance. And not just any someone—Gray. The silent but deadly operative on the Shadow Ops Team who often seemed far too aware of her. She'd be flitting around headquarters, juggling multiple tasks for her boss, and he'd suddenly step in. Grab the heavy box of supplies she was carrying. Open the door for her. Pin her in place with that dark gaze as he asked if she needed help.

And now he was carrying her into the hospital like she was his, holding her carefully in his arms like she was something special. Someone to be cherished.

He'd been at the coffee shop, she suddenly remembered. Watching over them. Lena and Kaylee had gone back inside to order another drink, and Gray had hovered near the front doors. Lena began trembling, remembering the men who'd cornered them in the back hall. Kidnapped them.

The sound of sirens grew louder, and she saw two police cars pulling up, the officers jumping out. Jett's voice was barking orders from somewhere, and Lena blinked in confusion. It felt like everyone was arriving at once, a million different things happening. Her head began to pound as she saw nurses rushing out the door to meet them, and then she slumped over in

Gray's arms, her mind trying to protect itself from all she'd endured.

Chapter 1

Two weeks later

Lena crossed the sleek lobby of Shadow Security Headquarters, her high-heeled boots clicking on the polished floor. The sound echoed throughout the empty lobby, the large windows showing nothing more than the dark sky outside. The building was staffed twenty-four-seven by security, but no one was at the receptionist's desk at this late hour. No doubt there were analysts and IT staff at work elsewhere in the building, as well as employees who were on shift work. It was quiet here out front though. Almost too quiet.

She slid her designer purse higher on her shoulder, moving toward the stairwell leading down to the basement. Her boss, Jett Hutchinson, was the owner and head of Shadow Security. As his personal assistant, Lena ran errands for him, booked flights and coordinated his schedule, and helped occasionally at his large home. With Jett's recent marriage to Anna and their new baby, Lena found herself coordinating with their nanny as often as she dealt with Jett's multiple business contacts. She was efficient and organized, however, keeping her busy boss on task.

Her phone buzzed in her purse, and she pulled it free, almost relieved someone was calling her. The silence surrounding her somehow almost felt ominous.

She shook her head, glancing down at her phone. She was being silly. Shadow Security was one of the safest places to be.

"I'm almost there," she told Jett after she'd swiped the screen to answer.

"Perfect. Let me know how much high-caliber ammo we have. One of my shipments was delayed in transit. Anna has been good at tracking our inventory since she came onboard, but with the baby and her newest pregnancy—"

"She doesn't have the current figures. It's fine," Lena assured him. "I'll update you on what we have. Anna's got her hands full with the baby—no doubt with you, too," she deadpanned.

"Very funny," Jett muttered. "Just let me know when you've got the numbers. Some of the guys are moving out soon, and I've been distracted as of late. I want to make sure they're fully equipped for their op. I keep saying we need to bring on more men—"

"And it hasn't happened yet," Lena finished. "We could put up job postings. You may have brought on men you know for the Shadow Ops Team, but you've got connections. I have no doubt you could easily bring in more quality team members. We can post listings on the classified jobs sites."

"I know, I know," he grumbled. "It'll happen at some point. I've got enough going on at the moment, however, to worry about screening new personnel. Call me back with the numbers. I've got another call coming in."

"Will do," Lena said, the phone line going dead.

Gruff and intimidating, Jett was a force to be reckoned with. Lena knew most people wouldn't joke with him the way she occasionally did. Lena, however, had seen it all. She and Jett went way back, and when he'd formed his own security firm and asked her to come onboard, she couldn't say no. She did everything. Picked up his drycleaning. Scheduled the housecleaners. She dropped off lingerie and condoms at his home with the same finesse she used when booking travel for the team or making reservations at a swanky restaurant for Jett's meetings with government contacts.

Besides all that, the work Jett and his team did was important, crucial to national security. Lena might not have the same clearances he did, but she saw no issue with his men ridding the world of the evil that lurked in the shadows. All former Special Forces soldiers, the team took on jobs the Feds couldn't or wouldn't do. Jett was a man who got shit done, and Lena was often behind the scenes, keeping his life and operation running smoothly.

Of course, she'd ended up right in the thick of things with Kaylee. Nick's old flame had witnessed a leak of classified information and been on the run from several men impersonating federal agents. Nick had brought Kaylee back to New York to keep her safe. They'd found her anyway, kidnapping Lena along with their target. After the team had located them, Jarid Cronin and Kyle Levins had been taken out in the rescue operation.

Lena shuddered, thinking about the third man who'd escaped. She'd returned to work after a couple of weeks recuperating, but that didn't stop her from looking over her shoulder, wondering if he'd track her down. According to Jett, Ivan Rogers headed a large North American sex-trafficking ring. He'd taken a particular interest in Lena, claiming he was going to keep her all for himself.

She'd been lucky as hell to get away from him.

The Feds had raided the property after the incident, but he was already gone. Out there somewhere. Always on her mind.

Pulling open the heavy door, Lena descended the stairs. The basement of headquarters housed the armory, gun range, and fully-equipped gym. The men on the Shadow Ops Team were often down there training and preparing for missions. They were both silent and deadly, and she was thankful men like them were on their side. The good guys.

Clearly, none of the Shadow Ops Team members were here tonight. Jett would've asked one of his team to check numbers in the armory if that were the case, not send her over. The men were probably out with their women or cozy at home, content with their lives. Lena didn't date anymore, which suited her just fine. Relationships hadn't gone so well in the past. The only man on the team still single anyway was Gray, and he had demons just like her. Secrets. A past he wanted to forget. She could admit that Gray was attractive in a dark and dangerous type of way. He might not hurt her, but it was still best that she kept her distance all the same.

Lena shook her head once more, clearing her thoughts.

Her heels clicked as she moved down the empty stairwell. This wasn't the first time she'd been here alone late in the evening and no doubt it wouldn't be the last. She slowed her steps, listening for what, she wasn't sure. The building was inside a secure compound, surrounded by a gated fence, cameras, and security staff. Everyone inside was cleared. Employees needed to badge in to enter the front door and the various secure areas within the building. It wasn't like someone could just walk in off the streets and hurt her.

Inexplicably, she shivered.

Lena hurried the rest of the way down, moving into the basement hall. The lights were on, but it still felt secluded. Glancing left and right, she strode toward the armory. Lena quickly swiped her badge and typed in the code, breathing a sigh of relief when she was inside the secure space. The heavy door clicked shut behind her.

It was silly for her to feel rattled. She was safer here than most anywhere else.

Moving quickly toward the area Jett had instructed her, she scanned the labels, looking for the correct boxes. Lena tallied the types of ammo he'd needed numbers on, taking a couple of photos and notes on her phone. She almost wanted to laugh at the absurdity of it. One day she was buying flowers or pretty lingerie for her boss's wife, maybe even helping them to research daycares and back-up nannies, and the next, counting bullets. Life was weird.

She scanned over the numbers she'd saved once more. Lena would shoot him a text as soon as she had cell reception again. The armory was a secure space with thick, metal walls. There was a secure line available to use, but a cell wouldn't work. She'd call Jett before she left headquarters to make sure that was all he needed. It had already been a long day, and she didn't want to come back again even later if she'd gotten the wrong information.

Giving the boxes of ammo one last cursory glance, she slid her phone into her handbag. Lena crossed the large space and opened the heavy door. Lena made sure it locked behind her, double-checking that it was secure, then shrieked in surprise as a man she didn't recognize came out of the gym across the hall.

"Whoa, easy there," the guy said with a grin, not bothering to slow his step as he approached her. "I didn't mean to scare you. I saw you head into the armory earlier."

"Oh," she said, taking a step back without thought, her heart racing. She was now almost pressed against the armory door, and her gaze inadvertently darted to the stairwell. She thought the man was one of the new IT guys, but why he was here in the gym so late, she didn't have an answer for. Was anyone else even downstairs right now?

"I've seen you around," he continued, not seeming to even notice her fear. "I wanted to introduce myself." His gaze slid to her hand. "I don't see a ring on your finger. Tell me you're single," he said with a lazy grin, edging slightly closer. Lena didn't miss the way his eyes flared with interest as he appreciatively looked her over. The guy still hadn't even told her his name.

"No. I'm not married, but I don't date. Jett's expecting my call, so I need to get going." She pushed away from the door, trying not to brush against him since he stood so close to her, then yelped in surprise as the guy's big hand landed on her arm, his fingers closing around her flesh.

Her pulse skittered, her breath hitching as she froze in place.

"Hey, wait—" he said.

Lena's frantic eyes slid to the door of the gym as another man came hustling out at the sound of her cry. He looked pissed as his narrowed gaze took in Lena and the man gripping her arm, but she was too happy to see him to care. A sweet sense of relief flooded through her, her entire body relaxing just a fraction.

"Gray."

Her voice sounded breathier than usual, shaky. She tugged her arm free as the guy from IT whipped around to look at who'd approached.

"Are you okay?" Gray asked, his voice a low rumble as he moved toward them with a frown. "I heard you scream."

Flustered, Lena felt her face growing warm. The last thing she needed was to look weak and incompetent again in front of the gruff former soldier. She already felt out of her element sometimes dealing with the work Jett and his team conducted. Sure, she might look organized and capable, but they were more adept at handling the dangers of the world than she'd ever be.

"I'm fine. He startled me when he came out of the gym. I didn't think anyone else was down here." She cleared her throat, both loving and hating the intense way Gray was watching her. "He grabbed my arm before I could walk away." Her voice faltered, and she knew in that instant that Gray saw right through the brave façade she was trying to put up.

"Move aside, asshole," Gray said, fisting the guy's shirt and yanking him away from Lena.

"Hey, what the hell, man? I just wanted to get her number."

Gray was already guiding her to the stairwell, giving the guy a scathing look over his shoulder. "You don't fucking touch her." His voice was deadly, brokering no argument. His eyes fell on one of the security cameras in the hallway, aiming in their direction. Gray pointed at it with his free hand, clearly knowing West Renkin, their IT guru, or someone in security would be monitoring it. "That guy needs to go."

Gray yanked open the door to the stairwell, guiding Lena ahead of him. Gray's astute gaze was already scanning over her as he took her upstairs, the man they'd left behind clearly no threat to him. No longer a potential threat to her. There was no way Gray would've turned his back to the guy if he thought otherwise.

Lena knew she probably looked terrified. Her heart was still beating a million times a minute, her palms felt slick, and she was sure her face was currently pale. She felt shaky as they began walking upstairs, suddenly realizing that Gray's muscled arm was lightly wrapped around her, giving her support.

She didn't feel scared with him, however, like when the other man had grabbed her arm. Instead, she simply felt...safe.

"Who the hell was that guy?" Gray asked, the deep timbre of his voice winding its way inside her. She remained pressed against his side, simply trying to focus on putting one foot in front of the other. She wobbled in her heeled boots, and Gray's arm tightened around her. His entire body was tense, on-edge, and she tried to absorb some of his strength. He was angry on her behalf, yet barely anything had happened. Embarrassment washed over her.

"One of Jett's new hires. I forgot his name."

"He won't be working here long," Gray muttered.

Lena didn't argue. She had plans to tell Jett about the incident herself, but she could sense that Gray was going to have words with their boss as well. Accidentally scaring her was one thing, but grabbing her arm so she couldn't walk away? She'd been paralyzed, taken back to—she shuddered, the memories nearly overtaking her.

"Are you okay?" Gray asked more gently, ducking his head lower. She was average height for a woman, taller in her heeled boots, but Gray was still bigger than her. Stronger. He'd been working out and was dressed in gym shorts, a tee shirt, and sneakers, but Lena knew he was positively lethal. Gray wouldn't have needed a weapon to take on that clueless guy from IT—or anyone else, for that matter. The Shadow Ops Team members were all former Special Forces soldiers. Just because they didn't wear a uniform anymore didn't mean they were harmless. Far from it.

"I'm okay, just rattled." Her voice still sounded thin. Lena sucked in a breath, trying to steady herself. "I shouldn't have gotten so shaken up over that. It just reminded me...."

"I know." Gray's quiet voice soothed something deep inside her. He wasn't overly talkative or pushing her for information. He was simply there, literally holding her up as he escorted her away. "Shit. Why would Jett send you here at this hour?" His voice was gruff, and he seemed unhappy that she was alone downstairs so late. While Shadow Security employed both men and women, the fact of the matter was, most employees were male. Lena wasn't a trained operative. She was Jett's personal assistant. She ran errands. Made appointments. And she hated how vulnerable she felt at the moment because of a seemingly small thing. It's not like she'd been attacked. A man had cornered her, not even realizing she was scared.

Her stomach churned.

"Jett needed me to inventory some ammunition."

Gray muttered a curse. "I could've gotten that for him."

"Guess he didn't know you were here," she said lightly, hastening a glance his way. They'd reached the lobby, and she faltered, her gaze landing on the windows and darkness outside.

"I'll walk you to your car." His voice brokered no argument. "Let's get the numbers to Jett first. I want a word with him anyway."

"Okay."

Gray was already calling Jett as they moved to the empty area behind the receptionist's desk, his phone at his ear. "Some asshole grabbed Lena just now," Gray said without preamble, the irritation clear on his face. He was still looking her over, seemingly trying to make sure she was truly okay. Gray yanked out a chair, guiding her to sit down, and she gratefully sank into it. "He cornered her against the door to the armory. I was downstairs in the gym and—yep. Got it." He set his phone down on the counter. "He's calling security to pull up the feed. Jett will call us right back."

Lena blew out a breath she hadn't realized she'd been holding. "What else did he say?"

"The guy's done here. Security will escort him out."

She stilled, worry suddenly coursing through her. Her gaze darted to the stairwell they'd just come from.

"What's wrong?" Gray asked, surprisingly attuned to her emotions.

"What if he's mad? He was trying to stop me from leaving, but it's not like he attacked me or something. He could sue the company for wrongful termination," Lena explained.

Gray's gaze narrowed. "You're worried that asshole might be mad at you?"

"Well…."

"He won't bother you again. Jett has lawyers. There are cameras in the hall. When I came out of the gym, you looked fucking terrified. He had his hands on you." Gray's voice was thick, and she couldn't read the different emotions dancing in his eyes.

"I was too scared to move," she admitted.

"There you go. No need to lose sleep over a dick like that."

Lena huffed out a laugh despite herself and didn't miss the way Gray's own lips quirked. They were full and positively kissable, and why she was thinking that at this completely inappropriate time, she had no idea. Gray could be gruff and somewhat of a loner. He kept himself slightly apart from his teammates, yet Gray seemed to notice everything about her tonight. It was both flattering and unnerving.

"Yeah. You're right," she finally relented. Lena licked her own lips, looking around the small reception area. Gray grabbed a water bottle for her, twisting off the cap before he handed it over.

"Drink this."

She nodded and gratefully took several sips. Gray's eyes were still on her, and she fumbled with the bottle as she tried to put the cap back on a moment later. With all of his attention and focus directly on her, she was flustered. Uncharacteristically so.

Despite the fact that he'd literally held her in his arms after the team rescued her, things had essentially returned to normal between them. And if she was far too aware of him whenever he was near? Well, she'd have to pretend he was simply another colleague, not the type of man who made her heart skip a beat.

Gray's phone buzzing on the counter made her jump, and he swore. "Hey boss. Yep. She's right here. I'll escort her to her car." His gaze landed on her again. "Lena. Do you have the numbers for Jett?"

"Of course," she said, opening her purse. She swiped the screen on her phone, pulling up the message she hadn't yet sent.

Gray easily relayed the info to their boss, confirming the numbers before ending the call. "I told Jett I'd get you out of here before security comes through with that asshole from downstairs. Jett will touch base with you later on but knew you were shaken up and probably wanted to leave."

"How? Oh. The security cameras." Heat washed over her face. For a normally capable woman, she'd let herself get spooked rather easily tonight. She knew Jett wouldn't hold it against her, but she wasn't sure if she liked Gray seeing her vulnerable side yet again.

He turned, grabbing a second bottle of water. Lena couldn't help but stare as he took a swig, noticing his thick biceps and broad shoulders. Geez. Even his hands look strong, with veins trailing across them. Thick fingers. Muscled forearms. A guy like Gray could really hurt a woman if he wanted.

Yet he'd physically pulled the other man away from her instead. Kept her safe.

Lena shivered.

"Let's get you out of here," he said more gently. "Are you okay to drive home?"

She looked up at him in surprise. "Of course. I'll be fine," she added, which somehow made her sound less certain. Steeling herself, Lena grabbed her purse and slung it over her shoulder, her heels clicking on the smooth floor once again as they walked to the doors. She looked polished and pulled-together but felt almost prim and prissy compared to Gray. He was athletic and muscular, confident and strong. Gray could annihilate any harm that came their way in an instant. She was just...Jett's personal assistant.

"I'll go first," Gray said, pushing open the door and stepping into the well-lit area in front of the building. The gesture was unnecessary but somehow made her heartbeat speed up just the same. He was protecting her even now, even if they were in no immediate danger. Had anyone ever watched out for her so carefully before?

Gray's gaze was scanning the mostly empty parking lot as she followed him outside. She could see the gated entry in the distance. The secure fence. And the dark forest that surrounded the secluded property.

"I'm parked right over there," she said, nodding toward her vehicle in the first row.

Gray waited for her to fall in step beside him, matching his long stride to her own. He didn't seem at all bothered by the cold winter air. She could smell his clean, masculine scent, mixed in with a trace of sweat. He'd started a workout before he'd rushed to her rescue, but the scent wasn't unpleasant. Gray was pure male. Rough and raw and real. Strong in a way she'd never be. The man had demons, no doubt, but he hid them well. Gray was the type of man who kept to himself, even amongst his friends. Funny that she was somewhat of a loner, too. She did her job and went back to her small home. The solitude was fine. Calm and quiet and truly all that she needed. Lena didn't want a man getting in her way, even someone silent, steady, and sure like him.

Gray didn't speak until they'd reached her vehicle. "You've got my number," Gray assessed, looking down at her in that intense way of his.

"Of course. I have the entire teams' numbers programmed into my phone."

"Call me if you have any trouble."

Her lips parted, but no words came out.

"Jett will have security let the asshole from IT know to leave you alone, but…." He nodded at her, his dark gaze intense. "Give me a call if there's an issue."

"Okay. Thank you," she finally added. Had she thanked him earlier? She wasn't sure. The entire evening was somewhat of a blur of frazzled nerves and spiked adrenaline. Lena wasn't usually like this. She prided herself on being professional. Poised and unfazed by anything. She'd been frightened down by the armory, but Gray also shook her up somewhat, leaving her scrambling to right herself. Everything he said threw her off, none of it ever what she expected.

"You're welcome." A beat passed as they stood there. There was no need for him to remain, yet here he was.

She swallowed, nervous for some reason, and grabbed her key fob from her purse, clicking the remote. Gray reached down, pulling open her car door, and goosebumps erupted over her skin at the chivalrous gesture. Gray watched her get into her vehicle, nodding at her once as she closed the door. He was going to watch her leave, she realized. Heat washed over her face as she started the engine and pulled on her seatbelt. Gray's eyes on her were unnerving. He didn't miss anything. Her hands were trembling slightly as she put them on the steering wheel, but she wasn't sure if it was from the fright she'd had earlier or her body's surprising reaction to the man standing just outside her car door. Trying to keep her composure, she checked her mirrors and backed out of the space, giving him a silly little wave before she drove off.

Gray was still standing there, arms crossed, as she headed to the gate, looking like a sentinel on duty, making sure nothing and no one harmed her under his watch.

Chapter 2

Gray awoke with a start, twisting in his sheets, his entire body covered in a fine sheen of sweat. The still air in his bedroom felt confining—oppressive. He'd forgotten to turn on his ceiling fan or crack a window. Somehow, the flow of cool air over his skin reminded Gray that he was free—half a world away from his captors. Thousands of miles away from his hellish days of torture.

He'd been in anguish in his nightmare, fighting with his abductors in the dark, blindfolded and restrained, unable to move away from the pain they were inflicting on him. The lashings. The beatings. The sheer brutality of the hatred bleeding from them.

Gray huffed out a shaky breath, the racing of his heart finally beginning to slow as he took in the darkness of his bedroom. The silence. The complete stillness. His gaze tracked to the clock.

Oh-two-hundred.

He sat up, swiping a hand over his face, and stiffening slightly with the movement.

The scars he bore on his back were a constant reminder of the whippings he'd received. The torture he'd endured. Three fucking days in captivity, and it had felt like a damn lifetime, the pain excruciating and never-ending. And Gray hadn't even received the worst of it. They'd captured another man as well—a Brit—who'd been slaughtered right in front of him. Was Gray more valuable to the terrorists because the U.S. flag had been sewn on his uniform? It didn't make sense that he'd lived while another man had died, but then again, nothing about war was just or fair. Not the way the op had gone south. Not the hostage situation. Not the sheer brutality the kidnappers had shown to their fellow man.

Gray and his teammates had gotten out of the Army after his rescue, with Jett forming Shadow Security. While Gray had been reluctant to join the team and was the last man onboard, he'd come to realize this was his calling. They took on operations the government couldn't or wouldn't do. Rid the world of evil men. Righted wrongs. Saved countless lives.

He couldn't deny the training the U.S. Army had given him paved the way for the missions the team conducted today. And wasn't that fucking priceless. They'd been in no hurry to save him from hell, so he'd left without so much as a glance back.

Gray's bare feet hit the floor as he swung his legs off the bed, and he sat there in the darkness, suddenly wide awake.

"Fuck," he muttered quietly.

The incident with Lena earlier tonight had rattled

him. She'd looked so fucking scared standing there, backed against the door to the armory. That prick hadn't even noticed she was frightened. Hadn't even considered she didn't want anything to do with him. Gray had seen her fear in an instant—the wild look in her eyes, the paleness of her face, the pulse jumping in her slender neck. She'd been fucking trembling as he'd taken her back upstairs, his arm loosely wrapped around her. The guy might've done no more than grab her arm, but it had terrified her. It had been all Gray could do not to pull her into his arms and assure her that he'd keep her safe.

He didn't do relationships, but hell. Something about Lena got under his skin. They felt like kindred spirits, in a way, even if she didn't realize it. Jett had confided to him once that he'd helped Lena with a bad situation years ago—an ex that was stalking her. Gray didn't know the details, and Jett had never uttered another word about it, but Gray could tell she was still slightly haunted. Lena was careful to keep her distance from the others and her private life private. No doubt it was for her own self-preservation, something he knew all too well.

And after her kidnapping two weeks ago?

Hell. No doubt that ordeal had given her a whole host of nightmares.

He could still feel the weight of her lifeless body in his arms. Recall the paleness of her skin, the weakness of her pulse. He'd wanted to hunt down the man who'd harmed her, but his priority at the time had been rushing Lena to the hospital. His teammates had swarmed the home, and that fucker had escaped.

Lena's shriek of surprise had him tearing out of the gym earlier. And when he'd seen that asshole touching her? Gray had been filled with rage. He'd wanted to punch the guy, pin him against the wall to show him exactly how it felt to be restrained and helpless. Lena had been too frightened to even move, and he hated that for her.

"Damn it all to hell," he muttered, standing up. The sheets fell to the ground, twisted up just like his insides currently felt, and Gray walked naked across his bedroom. His muscles bunched with the movement, his cock swinging free. Clothes felt too damn confining sometimes. Restrictive and unwelcome. Unless he was on an op with his teammates, when he'd sleep in his boxers, he preferred wearing nothing at all to bed.

He scrubbed a hand over his jaw, wondering if Lena was asleep right now—wondering what she wore to bed every night. His cock twitched, his blood suddenly rushing south. Lena was beautiful and sexy, with dark eyes and silky long, dark hair. She always wore stylish clothes, classier than he'd ever hope to be. She wouldn't be caught dead in the flashy things Anna often wore. Jett's wife loved attention. Lena was happy to stay out of the limelight but was classically beautiful. Her attractive, slim figure couldn't be hidden by her stylish attire. She had curves in just the right places—breasts that swelled against her tops, curvy hips, and an ass that he'd love to grip in his hands as he pulled her close.

Hell. Even her scent was enticing—some type of wildflower. Exotic. Sexy. Free. He wanted to bury his nose in her neck, inhaling some of her goodness, and then let his hands roam everywhere, making her moan his name.

Gray shook his head. That would never happen.

His cock was already half-hard just thinking about her, but he ignored his body's reaction. Lena could easily get a rise out of him—both literally and figuratively. He was more than happy to jump to her defense, and physically? She was fucking perfection.

Gray strode down the familiar hallway to his kitchen, not bothering to turn on a light, and poured himself a cool glass of water. After a nightmare like that, it would be hours before his mind could settle enough to enable him to fall asleep again. Ironic that he'd momentarily forgotten about it as his thoughts had turned to his pretty colleague.

His eyes scanned his dark kitchen, the digital clock on the microwave and stove looking brighter than usual in the middle of the night. Surprisingly, the darkness didn't bother him in his own home. Gray's senses were honed enough that he'd know if someone else were there. And while his Glock was locked in a safe, he didn't need a weapon to disarm a man. Gray had killed with his bare hands before, and he'd do it again, if necessary, the will to survive paramount above all else. Nothing mattered more than his freedom.

He took another swig of water, the cool liquid seeping down his throat but not stopping the torment of memories now resurfacing. He'd screamed in agony during his torture, no longer able to keep his cries silent no matter how stoic he'd tried to be. His throat had been red and raw when he'd finally been rescued, his back bloodied, his body bruised, his ribs broken. Jett had later told him he'd looked haunted— the same way Lena had appeared tonight. She might not have bruises on her porcelain skin, but she was tormented just the same.

Finishing his water, Gray strode back to his bedroom, unplugging his phone from the charger. He swallowed as he keyed in the code.

Bingo.

West had already gotten back to his earlier text.

West: Ran another check on the new guy. Nothing came up.

West: He's an ass but mostly harmless. Assuming Lena wouldn't agree with that.

Gray thumbed back a response.

Gray: Appreciate it.

There was a text from Jett as well, informing Gray that the new employee was no longer working at Shadow Security. Relief flooded through him. The man had frightened Lena, essentially trapping her against the armory door, and that was unacceptable.

Gray huffed out a breath and scrolled through his contact list, pausing on Lena's name. It was the goddamn middle of the night. He shouldn't bother her. Most sane people were sleeping at this time. The late hour didn't quell the urge Gray had to check up on Lena anyway. He'd driven past her place when he'd left Shadow Security earlier, noting that her car was parked in the driveway. The neighborhood had been quiet. Serene. He'd watched her home for a few minutes but seen nothing amiss, then come back to his own place.

She'd probably be pissed to know he'd looked up her address. Lena seemed to be the type of woman who valued her independence. She didn't date, as far as he knew, and kept her private life private. The woman clearly had a spine of steel to stand up to their boss. Jett would roll right over some people with his gruff demeanor. But Lena? She did her job and didn't let a damn thing faze her.

Until tonight.

He pushed the message icon, thumbing a text to her.

Gray: Hey. It's Gray. I had West run another background check on the guy. He's clean and shouldn't be bothering you.

Gray was shocked as his phone buzzed almost immediately.

Lena: Thanks. Jett told me he's no longer employed by Shadow Security.

Gray: Yep. He texted me earlier. Sorry if I woke you.

Lena: No worries. I couldn't sleep. Guess you might understand that.

Gray didn't answer right away and was still staring at the message when his phone buzzed again.

Lena: Sorry if I'm bringing up bad memories.

He hesitated, his eyes scanning over her text. Gray didn't need to burden her with his own problems. While his teammates were aware of his nightmares given that they deployed on ops together, he didn't need to cause Lena any additional strife. She already had enough to deal with given the kidnapping.

He was thumbing a reply before he thought better of it.

Gray: I'm usually up at random hours.

Gray: Why couldn't you sleep?

Lena: Bad dream. Then I thought I heard something outside.

He was calling her before he thought twice, already moving toward his bedroom. The line rang as he pulled on his boxers and jeans, his bare back reflecting in the mirror as he glanced over his shoulder. Scars crisscrossed his flesh. He shifted slightly, his muscles bunching with the movement. He was in top physical shape, but nothing could change the horror his body had been through.

Fucking terrorist assholes.

The phone rang again, leaving Gray to wonder if Lena was going to ignore his call.

Suddenly her voice was on the line, causing something in his body to awaken. He was still shirtless and barefoot in his bedroom, but his cock twitched against the confines of his boxers at the sweet sound of her voice. Adrenaline spiked through his veins, every muscle in his body now tense.

"I'm okay," Lena said as she answered.

"Are you sure you're okay?" he questioned. "It's the middle of the night. What did you hear?"

"I woke up after a bad dream and then thought I heard footsteps. It's probably just my overactive imagination." She tried to hide the slight wobble in her voice, and Gray felt his chest clench. She'd been spooked by whatever she heard. By whatever haunted her dreams.

"I'm coming over." He ended the call, something immediately settling inside him. He'd make sure Lena was okay and that her property was secure, and then be on his merry fucking way. If seeing her right now helped calm something inside his own restless mind, so be it. It's not like he'd be falling back asleep anytime soon. Making sure Lena was safe was better than dealing with his own nightmares.

After yanking open his dresser drawer, he pulled on a tee shirt. Gray didn't bother with a coat, just strode to his closet for a pair of boots. The night air bit into him as he went outside, but it was refreshing.

Cold and crisp. Anything was better than his memories of the dry, oppressive heat in the desert and sweltering inside the goddamn tent that he'd been held in. Blood mixed in with sweat and sand made for a miserable situation. And wasn't that the least of it.

Gray yanked open the door to his SUV and climbed inside, starting the engine. He'd been to Lena's exactly one time, earlier tonight, but he already had the directions memorized. He ran a hand over his shortly cropped hair, noting his own wild-eyed gaze in the rearview mirror. He needed to pull his shit together. If there was a problem, tearing over there like a bat out of hell wouldn't solve it. Something twisted inside him, however, at the idea that Lena was alone and scared. She'd stayed with Jett and Anna right after the kidnapping and probably wasn't used to being alone in her house again. He could understand that.

Ten minutes later, Gray was pulling onto her quiet street. Her neighborhood looked much like his own—homes on big, wooded lots and a serene sort of calmness in the surrounding area. Her road didn't have the cookie cutter look of some new housing developments. It was for people who sought privacy and peace, something Gray knew all too well. The fact that he and Lena were more alike than different wasn't lost on him. Sure, he was an operative trained by the U.S. military, gruff and muscular compared to her sophisticated appearance and polished movements, but deep down, he sensed they were more similar than he'd realized before.

His gaze swept the area before he shut off the engine. There was no movement in his headlights, but if someone was there, no doubt they'd be hiding now.

Biting back a curse, he stalked out of his car. Was he pissed about the situation or pissed he could never have a woman like the one he'd rushed to tonight?

Gray momentarily stilled as he walked up her driveway and Lena opened the front door, looking like a goddamn siren calling out to him in the middle of the night. The warm light from inside her home shone around her long, dark hair and pretty face like a fucking halo.

Lena was beautiful, vulnerable, and forbidden. His heart stuttered as he swallowed, tamping down all those feelings for good, and then Gray was moving toward her.

Chapter 3

Lena stepped back as Gray's gaze swept the front hall and living room. He'd grunted hello and then strode into her home like he owned the place. It should probably annoy her, but once again, she just felt safe in his presence.

"I don't think anyone's actually outside," she hedged. Why had she even mentioned to him that she'd heard something? Gray was exactly the type of man to rush over. All of the men on Jett's team were assertive, alpha males. Jett was the same. How Anna managed to deal with his overbearing tendencies was a wonder. Then again, Anna was a force in her own right. Their personalities might be different, but they balanced each other out. Jett doted on his wife, and it was sweet to see such a gruff man like him practically fall to his knees for his woman.

Not that Lena would take that type of chance in her own life.

She drunk Gray in as he stood in her foyer, taking in his tall, muscular body in jeans and a tee shirt. All of his muscles were on full display, and it made her heartbeat speed up. Gray was a good-looking man. She almost didn't know what to make of him standing here in her home.

"Maybe someone was out there, maybe not," Gray said in a low voice. "It's better to be safe than sorry given the circumstances."

She pressed her lips together and nodded. "You're right. Do you think someone might still be out there right now?"

Gray's dark eyes met hers. "If anyone was lurking outside, they probably ran the second I pulled up."

"Right. Of course." Maybe they couldn't see Gray's big frame in the dark, but knowing he was there and Lena was awake—or soon would be given his arrival—could've changed whatever plans they had. Maybe she was completely jumping to conclusions though. Just because she heard something after her nightmare didn't mean a thing.

"I'll check the yard and perimeter anyway. It should be easy enough to determine if anyone was out there before—trampled grass and the like. Footprints. I'll feel better knowing for certain that you weren't being watched for some reason."

"Me too."

Gray's long strides ate up the distance to the back of her home. He peered through her blinds into the dark night, his big hand separating the slats. Broad shoulders led to a muscled back and trim waist. And no, she wasn't staring at his toned ass. Not at all. She knew that he'd been tortured in captivity, but there was no evidence of that at the moment. He seemed nothing but virile and strong. Unstoppable. Still, her heart ached for him, knowing what he'd been through. Gray had a quiet confidence she appreciated, but Lena wondered if he'd always been this subdued. Was he a different man before his Army days? The answer was no doubt yes. Something like that would change a person.

"Is your backyard fenced in?" he asked, looking her way once again.

"Yes. There's a gate on the side, to the right of the house. It's not locked or anything, you can just undo the latch if you want to search the yard."

He nodded. "Wait here. I'll be back in a few minutes. I've got a flashlight in my SUV, and I'm carrying." Her gaze dropped to the weapon holstered at his waist. She hadn't even noticed it at first. It seemed like such a normal part of him.

"I'm sorry you had to rush over here in the middle of the night," she said, suddenly feeling foolish. This certainly wasn't the first time she'd woken up alone and scared. It was, however, the first time Gray had texted her right after one of her nightmares. That was nothing but a coincidence, but she couldn't deny she liked having him here, even if just for this one night.

Gray's gaze briefly swept over her, and Lena felt her blood heat. She'd thrown on a long cardigan over her thin tank and joggers. The night air had felt too cold as she'd opened the front door for Gray, the chill of it seeping into her bones. Ironic that he only had on a tee shirt. Winters in New York were no joke. There was no snow on the ground, however, and he'd only been outside mere moments. Certainly, he'd wear more suitable attire for extensive exposure to the elements. Even a muscular guy like him wasn't immune to the bitter cold.

"Do you need a jacket?" she found herself asking.

Gray looked surprised. "No. I'll be fine. I won't be gone long." He pinned her with a look, seeming to only now notice she was wearing what could pass as pajamas. Barefoot, she was even shorter than usual, making her feel feminine and delicate beside him. She crossed her arms, and his gaze briefly tracked to her breasts. Flushing, she was relieved when he glanced away. "Lock up behind me. I'll be right back." Gray was already moving toward the door, his gruff commands not anything she'd argue with. Lena had no intention of going outside.

She grabbed her phone and pulled up her doorbell camera footage. No one had been out front until Gray drove up. His movement in her driveway pinged a notification now, but she set her phone down. It would be weird to watch him through the doorbell camera, and the quality wasn't great anyway. She wished she had a camera out back, but even then, it's not like she'd confront an intruder. If Lena was ever truly in danger, she'd call 911.

She heard the gate opening outside but knew it was Gray. Her house felt empty and cold without him in here. Weird that she'd always felt relatively fine alone before—until her kidnapping that is. After a few minutes, Gray was back, rapping lightly at her front door. Lena opened it, then shivered as the cold air washed over her, her nipples pebbling beneath her clothes. She flushed, realizing she should've put on something more appropriate—or at least worn a bra. Too late now.

Somehow, Gray noticed her slightly panicked look. "It's okay," he murmured. "You're safe with me. Is it okay if I come in again?"

"Yes, of course," she said, stepping aside as she felt embarrassment wash over her. Something about Gray always had her feeling off-kilter. He seemed to always closely watch her, and her body reacted whenever he was near. While Lena could maintain her composure and professional decorum in the office, having him inside her home in the middle of the night threw her off. "Did you find anything outside?"

Gray cleared his throat as she locked the door behind him. "Not around your yard, but I found these in the driveway." Lena stilled as she stared at the zip ties in his big hand. Zip ties could be used for a lot of things. Binding cables or wires. Securing small items together.

They could also be used to restrain a person.

"Those were in my driveway?" she asked, realizing she sounded slightly hoarse. Lena was almost afraid to even ponder the implications of why they'd be there. He nodded. "That's…a little creepy, to be honest. I was out shopping earlier today, but I wasn't buying zip ties. And then I went into headquarters tonight, as you already know. What's wrong?" she asked, noticing the frown on his face.

"I'm just wondering how they got there. Several of them, at that." He paused a beat, seemingly trying to determine how to frame his next statement. "The investigation involving Ivan Rogers is still ongoing. He's seemingly disappeared without a trace. You've got a doorbell camera, right?"

"Yes. I can look through the footage. You really think he'd come looking for me? I'm not even sure if he knew my name. I was with Kaylee, so they took me, too." Her voice faltered, and she swore Gray's gaze softened.

"I don't want to rule anything out. Is there anyone else who'd have reason to seek you out or harm you?"

A flash of anxiety washed over her, goosebumps covering her skin. "Just an ex-boyfriend," she said, her voice weak. She straightened her spine at the concern on Gray's face. "He's in jail for other reasons. I'd rather not talk about it, but Jett can fill you in. I don't think he's someone I need to worry about anymore."

Gray slowly nodded, and she could practically see the wheels turning in his head. No one else from work knew about her ex, save for Jett. "We can make sure he's still locked up," Gray assured her. "I'll touch base with Jett in the morning."

"I doubt it's him," Lena said. "That was a long time ago."

Gray licked his lips, not looking convinced. "Check your camera footage to see if anyone suspicious has been outside your home. If someone was out there tonight, however, their movement could've been concealed by the darkness and not picked up."

Lena shuddered, and Gray's entire countenance changed. For such a gruff, macho man, he seemed surprisingly attuned to her. "Did you see any other signs that someone was outside my house?" she forced herself to ask. "Aside from the zip ties?"

"No. I searched your yard. I can check again in the daylight to be certain." She nodded, not trusting her voice as a fresh wave of fear washed over her. "I'm going to text Jett," Gray continued. "I don't think this has anything to do with the ass from IT, but it could mean someone else was watching you or your home. I'll get your ex's info from him, too, if that's all right. I understand if you don't want to talk about it, but we should cover all our bases."

She swallowed. "Okay," she agreed. The last thing she wanted was to drag Gray into that whole episode of her life, but she'd also told him the truth. Her ex was locked up, and it felt like their relationship and troubles had happened a million years ago. If anyone had been out there, she doubted it was him.

"Of course, it could be nothing," Gray said in a low voice, seemingly trying to reassure her. "The zip ties could've been from a neighbor working on a home project. Maybe they blew across the yard. Whatever you heard outside tonight could've just been an animal."

"Right, but it's better to be safe than sorry," she said, echoing his earlier comment.

"Exactly. I want to make sure you're not in any danger."

Her gaze briefly dropped to his full lips as his deep voice wound through her. Damn it. She didn't know who or what had been outside her home, and here she was staring at his mouth once more. Lena was far more attracted to Gray than she should be. His clean, masculine scent washed over her as they stood there, mixed in with a bit of spicy pine and smoke from being outdoors. Since moving here, she'd never once had a man in her home. Not even Jett. Now Gray was standing in her foyer, gruffly handsome and far more attractive than any man had a right to be. His hardened jaw and short-cropped beard were sexy as hell. As was the way his clothing hugged his broad shoulders and athletic build. Just thinking about those strong arms wrapping around her.... She wanted to shiver, but not in fear this time. Even when she'd awoken from her hellish ordeal of being kidnapped and drugged, she'd felt safe with Gray holding her.

"Well, thank you for coming over," she finally said. "I'm sure you're anxious to get home given the late hour—or early, depending on how you look at it. I should try to get back to sleep, too."

His gaze dropped to her hands, now clutched together in front of her. It's like he could see she was worried about being alone. "Why don't I crash on your sofa tonight?" Gray asked.

"You wouldn't mind staying here?" she asked in surprise.

"Of course not. It'll give me a chance to look around in the daylight, plus, I'll be here in case you hear anything else outside. You might feel more comfortable not being alone in your home."

She let out a shaky breath. "Okay. Thank you. I would feel better if you stayed."

"It's no trouble, Lena."

His deep voice made her insides twist around, knotting up with tension as she felt a familiar tug low in her belly. She liked the sound of her name on his lips far too much. She was also shocked by her body's reaction to him. While Lena had known Gray for over a year, he'd been in the background. She hadn't let herself get close to anyone at work, including him. Now, without even trying, he was edging past some of her defenses. All the tension and fear she'd felt earlier was slowly draining away with Gray right in front of her. Unable to stop herself, she yawned, her entire body suddenly exhausted from the weight of the day. Knowing he would be here overnight made her feel like she could actually relax and sleep for a bit, her entire body soothed by his presence.

"Get some rest," Gray gently ordered. "I'll be out here if there's any trouble. With my SUV in the driveway, I doubt anyone will be prowling around. They'll know someone else is here with you tonight."

"I've got a guest room and can put fresh sheets on the bed. That'll be more comfortable than the sofa."

He shook his head. "The sofa is fine. I don't sleep well anyway."

She stared at him for a beat, something unspoken passing between them. It felt almost intimate knowing he'd be staying in her home. She'd be tucked in her bed just down the hall, vulnerable as she slept. Lena wasn't scared though. Knowing Gray would be here had the exact opposite effect, and she was somewhat shocked as she admitted that to herself. Lena felt like she should say something else but finally nodded in agreement. "I'll grab you a blanket and pillow," she told him.

"That'd be great. Thanks."

As she turned to go fetch the things from her closet, she felt his watchful gaze on her the entire time. Lena felt her body heat, no longer used to a man paying such close attention to her. He wasn't leering, just…observant. She breezed in and out of the office at Shadow Security, getting her job done, without feeling flustered in the least. That wasn't the case tonight. Gray barely knew her, but somehow, he still saw too much, leaving her feeling somewhat exposed. Falling for a man like him could be dangerous. Sure, he might protect her physically, keep her safe and shield her from harm, but at what cost to her heart?

Chapter 4

Gray huffed out a breath, sinking down onto the sofa in Lena's living room. He'd tried not to stare at her earlier in the thin tank top and cardigan she wore, the soft material perfectly skimming over her womanly curves. He could see her nipples pressing against the fabric and the round fullness of her breasts. Lena had flushed as his gaze briefly tracked over her. She was gorgeous, yet sweeter and more vulnerable than she first appeared. Lena was always so closed-off at work, all business, and seeing another side of her made all of his protective instincts rise. He'd done his best to remain at a distance in the past, but there was no way he'd stand by earlier when some guy was harassing her at headquarters. And after her kidnapping mere weeks ago? He'd do everything in his power to keep her safe.

Gray rested his head in his hands as a torrent of thoughts churned in his mind.

Hell.

He didn't like that he'd found zip ties in her driveway, but then again, a few pieces of plastic could've easily blown through the neighborhood. Gray wasn't sure what had prompted him to offer to stay the night, but he'd hated the fear in her eyes at the thought of him leaving.

Gray lifted his head, looking straight down the hallway to Lena's closed bedroom door. Her trust in letting him stay in her home made his chest swell. Lena typically kept herself apart from everyone. She was Jett's assistant, and if she was around when they had gatherings, she was usually working, not relaxing with the team and their women. He'd often been unable to keep his eyes off her, taking in her sexy curves, pretty features, and beauty that made her glow from within. Lena was gorgeous, living up to the actual meaning of her name. Bright. Beautiful. The exact opposite of the darkness that filled Gray's life. Even his name was the color of gloom. It was an irony not lost on him.

Groaning, he wondered what his boss would think of Gray's spending the night at her home. Not that Jett's displeasure would've stopped him, and hell, the man would have no problem with Gray keeping her safe.

He rubbed the back of his neck, trying to relieve some of the tension he felt. Usually, when he woke from a nightmare, he'd be up for hours. Seeing Lena had distracted him from his own troubles, but now his thoughts were consumed with the woman down the hall.

Gray unlaced his boots, setting them neatly beside her coffee table. He removed his firearm, putting it beside his cell phone, then stood, moving to check that her front windows were secure. While he might like to leave a window cracked in his own bedroom to let in the cool winter air, there wasn't a fucking chance he'd take a risk with Lena's safety. Especially when no one knew where Ivan Rogers was.

He grabbed the pillow and blanket, stretching out on her sofa in the dark living room. The house was silent and still, but his thoughts wouldn't slow. Gray shifted around, trying to get comfortable, then stilled as he heard a soft cry from down the hall.

Shit. Was that Lena? He listened closely.

As more cries filled the air, Gray grabbed his firearm and was moving down the hall before he thought better of it.

"No!" she suddenly wailed.

"Lena!" He tried the doorknob, not surprised to find that it was locked, then burst into her bedroom as she cried out again, leaving the flimsy bedroom door in two pieces. Weapon aimed, he flipped on the light switch, his heart catching as he saw her twisted in her sheets, crying. His quick scan of the room showed they were alone, and Gray lowered his gun.

Another fucking nightmare.

Lena sat up in her bed, chest heaving, tears streaming down her face. Her dark hair was in disarray, and she swiped at her face, trying to brush away both long strands of hair and tears. Gray holstered his weapon, moving toward her, his heart thumping in his chest. "Lena." His voice sounded deeper than usual, and the urgency coursing through him was surprising. Lena was safe, but seeing her scared and crying gutted him.

She looked up at him, shaking, her breasts rising

and falling as they pressed against her thin tank top. Creamy cleavage briefly drew his attention, but his gaze tracked back up to her face, wet with tears. The haunted look in her eyes slayed him. "I had another nightmare," she whimpered, her voice breaking.

"I know." He sat at the edge of her bed and eased her to him, her slender body so small and delicate compared to his own. Gray wrapped an arm around her shaking shoulders, his other hand palming the back of her head as he guided her closer.

Lena clung to him, trembling, and buried her face in his chest as he tried to soothe her. It might be wrong for a thousand different reasons for him to be here in her bedroom, but Gray couldn't stay away if he'd tried. He breathed in her floral scent and felt the warmth of her body, his mind flashing back to two weeks ago when he'd carried her unconscious body out of the house of her captors. She'd been too pale then. Limp. Helpless.

And he'd wanted to murder Ivan Rogers right then and there.

"My nightmares are worse tonight," Lena finally said, her voice slightly hoarse from crying. "I was trying to forget what happened, but it's like everything is coming back to the surface."

Gray barely dared to move. Lena wasn't the type of woman to confide in him, revealing her fears, and her trust in him was everything. "I'm sorry," he said. "While I don't know all that you went through, I know it can be hell to relive moments you'd rather forget."

Their eyes met as she pulled back, and he hated how fucking lost she seemed. Lena clenched her fists, anger seeming to overtake her sadness as she drew in a breath. "I don't even remember half of what happened when I was in that home. I was drugged."

"I'm here if you want to talk," he said quietly. "You don't have to share anything you don't want to."

She bit her lip and nodded, another stray tear slipping from her eyes despite her anger. She swiped it away, determination filling her gaze. "I had a bad relationship years ago. An ex was stalking me," she explained as Gray stiffened. "He was controlling, dictating more and more what I could and couldn't do. I realized rather quickly he wasn't the type of man I thought he was, so I broke up with him. That's when he started following my every move. Stalking me. I was terrified until he ended up in jail for other reasons, but when Kaylee and I were kidnapped, it was like my very worst nightmare came true. I wasn't beaten or tortured like you, but it was torture all the same. The men after Kaylee, Cronin and Levins, handed me off to their boss. In a way, he was the worst of them all."

Gray's pulse pounded, his mind churning with scenarios he didn't even want to imagine. Things out of a woman's worst nightmare.

"He forced me inside the home and then drugged me and tied me to his bed," Lena said, her voice shaking.

Gray's hands fisted at his sides, rage boiling within him. "He assaulted you."

"Yes," she said matter-of-factly. "It wasn't exactly like you're imagining. He didn't rape me, although I'm sure he was planning on it. He liked that I was weak and helpless, and when I'd come to again, he'd grope me and tell me all the horrible things he was planning to do. I'd start to panic, and then he'd drug me again so I would pass out."

"Fucking bastard," Gray seethed. "I want to kill him for even touching you."

Lena wrapped her arms around herself, looking like she was trying to hold herself together. "I wouldn't mind. Is that horrible of me to think?"

Gray shook his head, his lips pressed together. If Gray had found Ivan Rogers in that home, the other man would've been begging for mercy. And Gray would've ended him without a moment of remorse.

"He was toying with me," Lena finally said. "I don't even remember most of it, but when we were in the SUV, the men were planning to sell the other women they'd kidnapped. I don't know where he was going to take me."

"He wanted to keep you," Gray said, his voice hoarse. He'd read some of Lena's statement to the police. Fuck. If they hadn't gotten there in time….

Lena reached over and grabbed his hand, surprising him. "I was so out of it, it almost feels like some sick, twisted nightmare. I keep trying to forget it even happened, but I'm terrified he's going to come back for me," she said, fresh tears filling her eyes.

"That'll never happen." Gray's voice was thick with emotion. "I'm already beating myself up for waiting outside the coffee shop while you went back in—"

"We've been over this," Lena interrupted. "No one was expecting them to track Kaylee down. Even if you'd come inside, you wouldn't have walked into the ladies' room with us. They were determined to get her."

"I could've waited in the hallway," Gray said, guilt

coursing through him. "By the time I realized you'd been gone too long…."

Lena shook her head, squeezing his hand tighter. "You found us. That's all that matters. Kaylee and I are both fine. Kaylee has Nick, and I stayed with Jett and Anna until I felt comfortable enough to come back home. We have to move on with our lives." She shrugged, swiping away another tear.

"You and Jett go way back," Gray commented, searching her face.

"We do. I've known him since before his military days."

"And you two never…?"

Lena shook her head vehemently. "Goodness, no. We've known each other forever. Old family friends. He's more like an older brother to me. When Jett got out of the military, he offered me a job at Shadow Security. How could I refuse? I was jumping around between various admin positions, and he pays me better than any of those ever could."

"He's lucky to have you."

Lena let out a huff of laughter. It felt good to make her smile, even if only for a moment. "That he is," she agreed, flashing him a tiny grin. "What time is it anyway?" she asked.

Gray looked over her shoulder to the alarm clock on her nightstand. "Oh-four-hundred. I've been here a couple of hours."

"Do you want some coffee? I'm not sure I can go back to sleep."

"Sure," he agreed, rising from the bed. "I doubt I'll fall back asleep either." He reached out a hand to Lena, enjoying the feeling as her soft, slender hand clutched his own. She rose to her feet, barely coming up to his chin. The baser part of him wanted to lower her back into bed and kiss away all those fears she had. Explore all that soft, creamy skin and then make love to her until she was clinging to him, crying out his name.

He could actually picture it happening, Lena's hair spilled out over the pillow, her gorgeous body beneath his own. It took everything in him not to duck down and kiss her soft lips right this second, running his hands over her perfect curves and admitting how much he wanted her.

"Thank you," Lena said, suddenly wrapping her arms around Gray in a big hug. He flinched as the material of his shirt rubbed against his back and immediately tried to hide his reaction.

"Did I hurt you?" she asked, the alarm clear in her voice as she pulled away.

Lena's eyes were filling with worry again, and Gray wanted to curse. The last thing he wanted to do was scare her off. "No. The fabric of my shirt caught against my scars. I'm fine." It was more than he'd ever shared with his teammates. Gray had no problem ignoring the pain when he knew to expect it. Donning a Kevlar vest or slinging a rifle across his back was uncomfortable sometimes, but his scars were usually a dull pain that he could live with.

Lena had surprised him, and he hated that his reaction had made her pull away.

She was warily looking at him now, her gaze tracking up and down his body, trying to see where he was injured. None of his scars were visible with his clothing on. Gray had enjoyed the pleasure of exactly two women since his Army days, and he'd fucked them without caring what they thought of his body.

He generally kept to himself now, not interested in a quick lay. He was too closed off to have a relationship, yet here he was, having no trouble with confiding in Lena. Taking her to bed was a privilege he'd love to earn. Thrashing around in his sleep because of his own damn nightmares, however, didn't exactly make him feel comfortable having a woman at his side while he slept. And wasn't that just another fucking thing the terrorist assholes had stolen from him.

"Are you sure you're all right?" she asked, her voice soft in the early morning hours.

"I'm fine." His voice was gruffer than he'd intended, and he reached out and drew her into his arms for the hug she'd wanted. His lips brushed against her temple, his immediate reaction to soothe her.

"I'm sorry if I hurt you," Lena said, her touch light. Gentle.

"You surprised me. In more ways than one." Gray released her and turned away before she could respond, striding down the hall toward her kitchen. Staying with Lena in her bedroom made him want all kinds of things he couldn't have.

Gray would protect Lena, even if it meant from himself.

Chapter 5

Gray frowned as he sat in the conference room several days later with his teammates. They were monitoring multiple situations, the most pressing being tracking down the man involved in Kaylee and Lena's kidnapping, Ivan Rogers. While the Feds had brought forth charges against him, the man had vanished. Raids had been conducted early this morning on his homes by Federal Agents and their foreign counterparts, but there was no sign of him.

The situation was far from over.

His mind drifted back to the weekend and the mysterious zip ties in Lena's driveway. Gray had gotten the name of Lena's ex several days ago from Jett, and true to her word, the asshole was locked up. Gray hadn't liked anything he'd seen in the ex's file: stalking, assault charges, domestic violence, battery.

His fists clenched.

Lena was lucky in the sense that he'd done no

more than stalk her before being arrested on charges stemming from previous incidents. That asshole wouldn't get anywhere near Lena while in jail, but she'd heard something outside her home. Was she just overly wary now because of the kidnapping and imagined she heard noises outside?

Gray had thoroughly searched Lena's property the following morning, finding nothing of use. She was as aloof and brusque as always now that they were back in the office. Few people knew about the incident from the weekend, aside from his teammates. Gray knew she was still somewhat shaken up from both the newly-fired IT guy grabbing her and hearing noises in the middle of the night, but she clearly managed to hide that fear from most people.

His gaze slid to the door as Lena herself briefly breezed in, handing Jett some papers. She looked stunning as always—flushed cheeks, rosy lips, and that dark, silky hair that he'd love to run his hands through. "These are from Anna. She said you needed copies but has the baby with her right now. She didn't want to bring Brody in here while he's fussing."

The harsh lines on Jett's face briefly softened. "She's supposed to be home resting."

"I think her exact words were 'the boss is a hard ass, and he needs this, stat,'" Lena said with a straight face.

Sam swiped a hand over his jaw, trying to muffle his laughter, but the other men's chuckles filled the room. "She's right," Luke quipped with a grin. "You are a hard ass, boss."

Jett shot him a look before thanking Lena for the papers, speaking to her briefly in a low voice. She turned, the high heels she wore showcasing her shapely legs. Her hips swayed in the pencil skirt she had on as she moved toward the door, and Gray swore his heartbeat sped up. He shouldn't be lusting after a colleague, but hell. Something about Lena just did it for him. She was sexy and smart with a slight vulnerability that called out to him.

His mind briefly drifted back to their breakfast together the other morning. After drinking coffee together in the hours before dawn, she'd cooked for him. Lena used to prepare meals for Jett all the time, so it shouldn't have surprised Gray as much as it did. The entire scene had just felt so damn domestic. Lena had pulled her long, dark hair back into a ponytail, making her appear younger than she was. She'd slipped off her long cardigan to cook, and Gray once again noted that the material of her shirt hugged her breasts perfectly, showing off their perfect swells. He'd done his best to be the perfect gentleman and not stare, but damn. They were a delicious handful, and wouldn't he have loved a sample.

Gray's eyes were glued to her ass in that slim pencil skirt as she walked out the door, before shifting back to his teammates around him. Of course, Jett had noticed him watching her.

Gray kept his own expression neutral. There was no reason to admit he'd been admiring her retreating figure. Lena was skittish. She was aloof and usually kept herself distanced from the others because of fear, not snobbery. He'd love to be the one to take care of her. Soothe her frayed nerves as he slowly undressed her, peeling away her layers of clothes and shields of defense. He'd get her to open up to him as he explored her gorgeous body. Touched her soft, satiny skin. She was the type of woman who would come alive under his touch. Wouldn't Gray love nothing more than to bury his face in her full breasts and then feast on her sweet pussy, listening to her mewls and cries as he devoured her. When she was good and ready for him, he'd thrust his cock in her slick heat, giving her what she needed. Taking what he wanted. Making her cry out his name and let go of her troubles as she surrendered to him.

His dick twitched as he clenched his fists. They had work to do, and here he was lusting after a woman he'd never have.

Jett cleared his throat as he moved to the front of the conference room. "West briefed me shortly before this meeting. As the team is already aware, Federal Agents and our foreign counterparts raided all properties owned by Ivan Rogers at oh-five-hundred local time today. He owns multiple homes, both stateside and abroad. Ivan was not among the men rounded up. The Feds are taking those found into custody as well as confiscating computers, electronics, and files."

"Why the hell didn't this happen before?" Nick asked, his expression livid. "Kaylee and Lena were kidnapped two weeks ago, and this guy Rogers has been on the wrong side of the law for years. He heads up a goddamn sex trafficking ring!"

"The charges brought forth against Rogers never stuck until now," Jett said, his gaze sharp. "He doesn't operate out of his private homes, and they couldn't obtain warrants to search the U.S. properties until late last night. Ivan typically hires lowlifes such as Cronin and Levins to do his dirty deeds. They worked out of rental homes, apartments, and the like."

"Fuck." Gray's fists clenched.

"It's unusual that Ivan involved himself in this directly," Jett said, his expression growing more serious. "According to Kaylee and Lena's statements, Ivan Rogers was the one driving the getaway car."

"Why?" Luke asked. "A guy like that heading up a huge operation must have hundreds of thugs working for him."

"It doesn't make sense," Nick agreed. "There's something very fucked up about this entire situation. Something we're missing."

"We believe Ivan was in New York because of several contacts in the city. With multiple trafficked women being temporarily held at a local home, he was here inspecting the merchandise, so to speak." Jett's voice was grim. "Driving the car when Cronin and Levins found Kaylee might've simply been a crime of opportunity for him."

"Motherfucker," Nick growled.

"All the women in the home were terrified," Sam said, anger crossing his own features.

As Gray recalled, there had been five other women in the room with Kaylee. Lena had been singled out and separated from the others. The most notorious man of them all had wanted her. Gray was thankful they'd gotten there when they did, but Ivan had still threatened Lena. Touched her. Drugged her. He felt sick thinking about the even worse things that could've happened.

"Some of those women were too scared to give statements, but at least one did. She was from a small town in upstate New York," Jett said. "She met a man online and traveled to the city to meet him. The man kidnapped and assaulted her."

"Jesus," Luke muttered.

"Kaylee said the men planned to assault them as well," Nick said, looking slightly sick at the thought. "When they were done using them, they'd be sold to the highest bidder."

"Fucking bastards," Ford said.

"Do I feel bad that Cronin and Levins are dead? Nah," Sam said, crossing his arms. "Not one bit."

"They deserved everything they got," Gray said, his voice hard.

"Ivan Rogers is extremely dangerous," Jett said, moving to his laptop and pulling up a picture on the big screen at the front of the conference room. He clicked a button, and a map appeared beside it, pinpointing the locations of Ivan's properties around the globe. "He has connections everywhere. These are his homes," Jett said. He pushed another button, and crisscrossing red lines, a messy web of trouble, appeared. "And these are the known locations his operation has trafficked women from so far. The Feds have asked for our help in locating Ivan and bringing him in. Let's get down to business."

***

An hour later, Gray's stomach was churning. "This guy's a sick fuck," Sam said, looking enraged. The men had seen a hell of a lot in their careers, but knowing innocent victims were being hurt by ruthless men never got easier. And Ivan was more twisted than most.

"I'd like to have five minutes alone with him," Nick muttered. "I'd beat him to a pulp and have him begging for mercy."

Gray's jaw ticked.

The man was pure evil. Ivan and his men had taken girls as young as thirteen and auctioned them off to foreign buyers. Some had eventually turned up dead, their bodies bloodied and bruised. Many of the victims had been lured online. Teenagers. College students. Women in their twenties and thirties. It had been a profitable scheme for Ivan, but it made Gray ill to know that Lena had experienced part of that dark, twisted world.

"Were his bank accounts frozen, boss?" Ford asked.

"Yes, the ones the Feds were aware of. It's likely he has money hidden offshore. Tracking them all will be difficult if not impossible. Given we're aiding in the search to find him, locating where the money is would be helpful. We're going to chase down other leads first."

"Do they believe he's still in the U.S.?" Luke asked.

"There's been no trace of him since the kidnapping. He wasn't inside the home when it was raided."

"Well, no shit," Gray muttered. "If I was him, I'd get the fuck out of there, too."

Jett turned toward the big screen. "While the women and girls trafficked were taken from multiple locations around the country, I'd like to focus on where they ended up. The Feds are currently reviewing his personal files and information stored on his computers, but as you know, we like to do things our own way. I've asked West to get the IT guys on Ivan's known travel. His preference is to use private jets, avoiding commercial airlines.

"Makes sense given he's trafficking women," Ford said.

"We're going to get the information on which companies and planes he used and scour the flight records. While he doesn't own a jet, he uses the same services frequently. He's also arrogant enough to book them under his own name."

"Why the hell hasn't the government looked into any of that yet?" Nick asked, looking irritated.

"The Feds move at a snail's pace," Gray muttered. "If they just raided the homes, it'll take weeks to move on this intel."

"And we're jumping ahead without them," Jett said. "We'll obtain the flight records and determine the most likely places Ivan is hiding out. If he's not in his private homes, Ivan is likely where his business is. He's still running his shitty enterprise and will need the cash with some of his assets now frozen. West is tracking the services he uses to book private jets. From there, we're going to determine what his most common travel destinations are. We'll narrow it down to determine where he most likely fled."

Sam was drumming his fingertips on the table, eyeing Jett. "We'll have to pose as buyers."

"Potentially. If he's selling women, he's going to be where the action is. Once we have city names, we'll narrow down specific locations. Ask questions."

"And then we'll grab that motherfucker," Gray said, a sudden surge of adrenaline spiking through his veins. While they'd been in the dark the past couple of weeks, the new intel on his use of private jets was proving to be timely. Ivan Rogers might be missing, but they'd determine where he was likely holed up,

move in, and bring that asshole to justice once and
for all.

Chapter 6

"Oh my gosh, I'm so sorry about this weekend!" Anna gushed, rushing over and enveloping Lena in a big hug. "Jett told me all about the creep who cornered you in the basement. Men, am I right? They all think they're God's gift to women. I'm so glad Gray was there to scare the shit out of him."

Lena pulled back, smiling despite herself. She wasn't surprised in the least by Anna's exuberance. Lena guided her away from where the receptionist, Clara, was currently talking on the phone with a client. "It was creepy," Lena admitted. "The guy had just started working here but claimed he'd noticed me around. He said he didn't see a ring on my finger and wanted my number."

"The nerve of him!" Anna said, her voice rising. "So what if you don't have a ring? You could still be in a relationship or not at all interested in an ass like him. What an absolute dick. That's the last thing you needed after what just happened to you and Kaylee. You've barely been back at work."

"Exactly," Lena said, shooting her a knowing look. "I'm glad he's gone. I don't think I'd have felt comfortable running into him at the office after that little encounter. Gray rushed out of the gym looking like he wanted to murder the guy."

Anna nodded, a look of glee suddenly crossing her face. "The guy from IT probably pissed his pants when that happened. Gray's a good guy but badass. I wouldn't want to run into him in a dark alley, you know what I mean?"

"Well, that's the absolute truth," Lena agreed. "He'd never harm a woman though."

"Of course not! I just meant if I was the bad guy."

Lena tried to hide her smile. The idea of Anna prowling around pregnant like some criminal in a dark alley was ludicrous. "Believe me, the guy was shocked when Gray yanked him away from me." She wrapped her arms around herself, remembering the feel of that guy gripping her forearm—and the instant terror that had coursed through her. "I'm not sure what he expected, but he was totally clueless. He didn't seem to think he'd done anything wrong, but cornering me in the basement to get my number was idiotic."

"Dick," Anna muttered, and Lena huffed out a laugh. It felt good knowing Anna was angry on her behalf. While the two women weren't very much alike personality wise, they'd become friends. They'd had lunch together, grabbed coffee, and of course spent time at the office and at Jett and Anna's large home.

"I just hope he doesn't scare some other woman like that. How are you feeling?" Lena asked, ready to change the subject. She glanced at Anna's baby bump.

Anna was showing earlier this time around and was positively glowing today.

"Good, but I've been so tired. I took a quick cat nap when the nanny was there earlier but then came in to the office. I'm convinced it's another boy," Anna said, running a manicured hand over her belly. "Wouldn't Jett love that? A house full of penises," she surmised as Lena choked back her laughter. "There's already too much testosterone around here as it is."

"I thought the nanny had Brody all day?" Lena asked, glancing over at the sleeping baby.

"She did, but I felt like I'd miss him too much, so I brought him into work and gave her the day off. It must be those darn pregnancy hormones. I'm either in tears, sleeping because I'm so exhausted, or begging Jett to take me to bed and have his wicked way with me," she teased, waggling her eyebrows.

Lena shot her a surprised look.

"Oh, honey, let me tell you—those pregnancy hormones make you want it all the time. Maybe not in the first trimester when I had morning sickness all day long, but now? I can't get enough of my man. I should set you up," Anna said, looking excitedly at Lena. "Just think, our kids could have playdates together."

"No way," Lena said, shaking her head. "The last thing I need is a man."

"Look, I know some of the story with your ex. Don't worry, Jett only gave me the barest details," Anna quickly added. "I realize that you're skittish for a very good reason. But not every man is horrible."

"They're not all bad, but I still don't need you to set me up," Lena said, flashing her a warning look. "I'm perfectly happy."

The door to the secure area opened just then, effectively ending the conversation as Jett and the rest of his team came walking out. Ford made a beeline for Clara, ducking down to give his own pregnant wife a lingering kiss. Luke and Sam were deep in conversation with Nick. Jett sauntered over to Anna's side, and Gray hovered at the edge of their group. He was often silently watching from the sidelines, Lena had noticed, and she blinked in surprise as she realized his focus was solely on her right now.

Lena met Gray's gaze and tried to tamp down her body's immediate reaction as he approached. Still, nervous butterflies fluttered in her stomach and heat coursed over her skin. She'd done her best to keep her distance this week, putting the past weekend behind them. It had felt intimate crying in his arms in her bedroom, but Gray was a colleague, not her boyfriend. She was embarrassed he'd seen her like that. Then she'd cooked breakfast for him like they were a couple or something.

Gray had come over last weekend to make sure she was safe. That was all.

"Hi there." His voice was a low rumble that practically sent a shiver snaking down her spine. He looked good today—too good. The cargo pants and black tee shirt that he wore showed off his muscles and strong physique, and she knew exactly how those muscles felt against her.

Lena felt her cheeks begin to warm.

"Hi," she said, immediately feeling flustered.

"You've been avoiding me this week." No pretense. Gray was blunt and to the point. His dark, short-cropped beard made him look rough-and-tumble, and the intensity in his eyes made her heart skip a beat.

He stood a respectable distance away, but she could breathe in his clean scent and feel the warmth of his big body. It felt like every nerve ending in her body was firing as she reacted to him. Her pulse pounded; her breath hitched. Even her voice wobbled as she answered him. "It's been a busy week."

He nodded. "It has. We're monitoring multiple situations and have another briefing this afternoon."

"I hear the Mexico mission is on standby," she said, swallowing. Gray's watchful gaze on her was unnerving. Maybe she'd flushed around him, felt his heated look as she'd moved around her kitchen and made breakfast, but nothing had happened. He'd checked her property after they ate, made sure she was okay, and left.

And she'd kept her distance all week.

Gray had literally broken her bedroom door down to get to her. He'd offered to replace it, too. While she was shocked, she also wasn't. He was former Special Forces, just like Jett and his teammates. And he'd done what he needed to get to her.

The conversations in the lobby continued on around them, and Lena felt like they were in their own little bubble, separated from the world. Gray knew she'd been steering clear of him, and it was obvious that he was done with her avoidance tactics.

"The mission is on standby until we resolve your and Kaylee's case," Gray told her, his eyes intense. "We have a little flexibility in the timing with Mexico, so Jett wants to handle this first. We just got some information that might lead us to Ivan Rogers."

"Oh really?" she asked, suddenly feeling worried. "Do you have a location?"

"Not yet, but we're narrowing down the possibilities," Gray said, clearly noticing her concern. "We think he flew to one of the areas where his sex-trafficking operation is run. Jett already told you his homes were searched."

Lena nodded, but a tinge of worry coursed through her. "He did," she said, her voice faltering. Tears smarted her eyes. "I think we'll all feel better when he's found," Lena managed to say.

"Are you okay?" he asked, his voice gentler.

"Just more bad memories," she murmured quietly.

Gray studied her for a moment, and it felt like he could see right through her. "I know about bad memories, hellish moments that live with you forever." Their eyes met, something passing between them. Gray hid his demons well, but she sensed that what he'd just told her wasn't something the others were privy to. No doubt they knew he'd been tortured, but the mental anguish he still dealt with? The thoughts that plagued him in the middle of the night?

Gray kept that shit locked up.

She shifted slightly, and Gray's eyes moved from her own, tracking down over her. She felt his gaze on her hips. Her thighs. Trailing down her legs to the high heels she wore. He looked ready to roll into battle, and she felt like a sexy secretary or something. Why couldn't she be strong like him? "You're braver than me," she said. Brave in his career choice, brave for approaching her. Gray and his teammates literally ran into danger. She'd panicked in the middle of the night.

He shook his head. "You're brave as hell, Lena," Gray told her. A beat passed as she searched his dark eyes. Nothing but sincerity shone within them.

"Oh, I meant to tell you—those zip ties you found were one of my neighbors," Lena said, grateful for a reason to change the subject. "A guy up the street was finishing his basement and had a number of supplies delivered. A couple of smaller items blew away in a wind gust. Another neighbor had plastic sheeting in her yard."

Relief crossed over his face. "That's good news. When did you find out?" His jaw ticked, and she could tell he'd been worried.

"Just this morning. I'm still not sure what I heard outside the other night, but at least the zip ties were nothing nefarious."

"I'm glad," he said.

"Me too. Oh, and don't worry about the bedroom door. I already had a handyman install a new one."

"Hell. I was going to pick one up this weekend."

"I know. I just feel safer when I can lock my door. I know it's silly since the house is locked."

"It's not silly at all," he countered. "And now I feel guilty for not doing it sooner."

"There's no need to feel guilty. It's already taken care of," she assured him. She cleared her throat. "I need to head downstairs. I'm helping Anna out with the numbers again and have to check the inventory for a few—"

"I'll go with you," he said abruptly, cutting her off. Her lips parted in protest. "It's no trouble, Lena." Once again, a shiver raced through her as Gray said her name. His deep voice calmed something inside her, and she definitely shouldn't like it as much as she did.

"There you two are!" Jett boomed, sauntering over

to them with Anna at his side, baby Brody in a stroller. "I'm taking Anna home for the day so she can rest. She should not have given our nanny the day off," he chastised, soothing Anna's frown with a brief kiss. "I'll be back soon. We're briefing at fourteen hundred."

"Got it, boss," Gray said.

"You'll help Lena downstairs," Jett said. It wasn't a question.

"Already taken care of."

Lena stiffened, not liking that Jett seemed to think she couldn't handle going back down there alone. Anna quickly jumped in, thanking Lena for covering for her yet again. "You might have to hire someone else when baby number two comes," Anna said sweetly, snuggling closer to Jett.

"Don't I know it. We need more admin help, more men on the Shadow Ops Team." He muttered a curse. "We're busy, which is damn good. I have to admit even I didn't expect Shadow Security to grow so quickly."

"Tell your brother to retire," Anna said with a wink. "I'm sure he'd love to join the team."

Jett barked out a laugh. "Slate? There's not a chance in hell he'd retire from the Navy to come work for me."

"Yeah, I don't see that happening either," Lena admitted. Jett's brother Slate commanded a SEAL team in Coronado. There wasn't a reason for him to give that up at this point in his career. The two men were complete opposites. Whereas Slate thrived on military order, Jett ran things his own way. Not every man was cut out to run black ops. Jett loved toeing the line, seeing how much he could get away with.

Lena had to admit, his team got shit done. She could hardly fault her boss for being on the right side of justice. Not when she knew of the evil that lurked in the world.

Jett eyed Gray. "You were the last guy I convinced to come on board. Who was that old buddy of yours that you hung around the pool halls with? You swore up and down he was one of the best damn snipers you've ever known."

Gray smirked. "Boone? I think he's out of the game, boss. And for good reason."

Jett pointed a finger at Gray. "I want his contact info. We've got a hell of a lot going on, but there's more on the horizon. It's about damn time I looked at expanding the group."

Gray's chuckle filled the lobby. "The day Boone joins the Shadow Ops Team will be the day hell freezes over, but sure, I'll pass on his contact info to you. I'll tip him off, too, so he knows that you're coming for him."

"You do that. We need the best of the best on the team. If you trust him, that's all I need to know."

Gray nodded, the two men exchanging a knowing look. Lena could hardly imagine what they'd seen while serving together but knew all of the men would lay down their lives for one another. Gray might be haunted by his past, but that hadn't stopped him from joining his teammates in more deadly missions. For running right into danger to save her.

As they said their goodbyes to Jett and Anna, Lena found herself heading toward the stairwell again, alone with the one man she felt safest with. Goosebumps covered her skin as Gray's warm hand landed at the small of her back. He reached out with his other, pulling open the door, the heat from his muscled body seeping into her skin.

"It's okay," he murmured as she hesitated for just a beat on the stairs.

"I know." Her voice was breathy again, but her nerves weren't from returning to the basement. Not at all. The shakiness in her voice had everything to do with the man behind her. She smoothed her palms over her pencil skirt, looking up to meet Gray's gaze.

Her stomach lurched, and Lena got the feeling that Gray knew all too well the effect he had on her.

The trouble was, she couldn't do anything to stop it.

Chapter 7

Gray's gaze trailed over Lena as they walked downstairs. Her dark hair swished behind her, the sexy floral scent she wore filling the air between them. He'd never been particularly chatty, but he kept to himself more than ever since that fateful mission. Maybe that was partly what drew him to this woman. Lena wasn't overly talkative either. She wouldn't pry him for details he didn't want to share about his captivity or ask him to recount memories he wanted to forget. Gray felt an odd sense of peace around her. It was strange considering he didn't actually know too much about her.

He did, however, know exactly what it felt like to hold her in his arms.

The more time Gray spent with Lena, the fewer reasons he had to stay away. Lena might think she was masking her emotions most of the time, but Gray saw the uncertainty she had. The very real fear she kept hidden beneath the surface. And damn if that defenselessness didn't call out to him even more. She wasn't helpless. Far from it. But while Lena might be independent, content to move through life alone, he didn't miss the flush on her cheeks when he was near. Gray affected her. Even now, her breath had hitched as his hand landed on the small of her back, guiding her toward downstairs.

Gray swallowed.

He liked the idea of keeping her close. He couldn't exactly spend the night with her even if he wanted to, not with the nightmares that tormented him. If Gray awoke, thrashing around and forgetting where he was, Lena couldn't be anywhere near him.

His fists clenched. All the more reason he kept to himself since his Army days. Lena was too good for a quick fuck. If he ever made love to her, he'd want her close all night, her naked body pressed against his own.

He could never risk it.

Noise came from the stairwell above them, and he glanced up, Lena looking back as well. Sam and Luke were ambling down the stairs, Sam with a shit-eating grin on his face when he spotted Gray and Lena together.

"What's up, buddy?" Sam asked with a smirk. Any other comments would no doubt be saved for later. Neither of the men would razz him about Lena with her standing right there. "Lena," Sam added, shooting her a smile.

"We're heading to the armory," Gray said. "Did you two miss me already?"

"Sorry, but Lena's way prettier than you," Sam joked. "And yes, I'm hella happy with Ava, just pointing out who we'd rather see down here."

"We're hitting the gym," Luke said.

Lena tensed ever so slightly, her mind no doubt on the other night. "I got the door," Gray said quietly, reaching around her to pull it open. He shot a pointed look at his teammates, and Sam's smile slid off his face. Both of them knew about the asshole from IT. It wasn't like the kidnapping she'd endured, but the man had put his hands on her.

"Is Anna feeling okay?" Luke asked when they were in the hallway. "Jett seemed anxious to get her home."

Lena frowned. "She said her morning sickness was better, but I think she's been really tired."

"Which is why we're down here," Gray said, his voice even. "Lena's doing some of the inventory, so we'll catch you guys later."

Lena kept close to him as they moved toward the armory door, and Gray hated that she was nervous. Briefly, Gray wondered what could've happened if he wasn't there the other night. Lena was a beautiful woman, and some men couldn't take no for an answer. Given that he was new here, he likely had no idea about the kidnapping. While the media had revealed that several women were being held inside the home, no identifying details about Lena or Kaylee were included.

He swiped his badge, keying in the code, and then they were moving inside the armory, the heavy door swinging shut behind them.

"Are you okay?" Gray asked as a brief look of panic crossed her face.

"Of course." But her hands were tightly clutching the papers she held. She took a deep breath, seemingly steeling herself against whatever memories were coursing through her mind.

Gray cleared his throat. "Would you rather I do the inventory alone?" he asked.

"No." Her eyes met his, pleading. "And don't tell Jett."

"Tell him what?" Gray said with a shrug. It was a casual movement, but he felt anything but relaxed. His entire body was rigid, his pulse pounding. Aside from the ass cornering Lena against the armory door the other night, she'd been kidnapped two weeks ago. Forced inside an SUV by Cronin and Levins. Tied to a bed by Ivan Rogers. While Gray thought she probably needed more time off to process everything that had happened, Jett said she insisted on returning to the office. She was strong as hell for coming back to work this soon. Gray knew what it was like to go on living when your entire world had been altered. Nothing was the same for him after he'd been tortured. His broken ribs and bruises had healed. The open cuts on his back were scars now, usually something he could ignore.

But the nightmares? The feeling of being trapped and helpless, unable to move? Those were tougher to deal with.

Gray didn't press her for additional details. If he didn't want to share his own memories of being held in captivity, why the hell would Lena want to tell him more than what she already had? She'd talk about it if she wanted to, and Gray would be here for her if that happened.

Lena sucked in a breath, accidentally dropping the papers she'd been holding, the sheets fluttering to the ground.

Gray crouched down, gathering them up for her. "Is this everything you need to inventory?" he asked, trying to turn her attention to something other than her memories.

She nodded, her expression unreadable. Lena was throwing up her shields again, pulling away. She reached out and took one of the papers from his hand. Sparks shot through him as their fingers accidentally brushed, and he could see her surprised reaction as well. He hesitated, half tempted to pull her close like he had the other night when they were alone in her bedroom. She looked like she was trying to hold herself together right now.

"Let's get started," she said, her voice shaky.

Gray tamped down his emotions and nodded before turning away, moving toward the section that housed the items he needed. "I'll start with everything on this page," he said, his voice husky. Fuck if he didn't want to pull her into his arms and wipe that fear off her face. He felt Lena's eyes on him, but he got to work, burying whatever needed to be said.

After a moment, he heard her movement, Lena checking the supplies on her list as well, making notes for what needed to be ordered.

"Do you really think you'll be able to find Ivan Rogers?" Lena asked after a few minutes. She'd gone still, and Gray's head swiveled in her direction.

"Yes."

"But how can you be sure? I'm constantly afraid he's out there somewhere, looking for me. I was stalked before by an ex, and it's a horrible feeling."

The rage Gray instantly felt burned hot and bright. If her asshole of an ex wasn't already rotting away in jail, Gray would go find the bastard himself. He tried to rein in his anger, keeping his voice calm as he reassured Lena that she was safe.

"Ivan Rogers doesn't know we have a lead on his private jet flights. When the Feds raided his properties, they were able to obtain the names of the contacts he used to book planes. Private planes. There are no flight records with his name on commercial airliners because he doesn't use them. That goes for the men working for him, too. West will hack into the flight records to determine his most frequent destinations. He doesn't know we're gathering his flight information," Gray reiterated, his voice low. "While Ivan Rogers no doubt realizes his homes have been searched, his business dealings have been hidden for a long time. He had a big network of men working for him. The Feds hadn't been able to get any charges to stick against him in the past. He was careful. Meticulous in his work, letting his men take the fall. It burns me up that he kidnapped you and Kaylee, but now we have solid evidence against him. We're about to find where his business dealings are and blow that shit wide open. Ivan Rogers' days are numbered."

She let out a shaky breath.

"What are you thinking?" Gray asked, trying to keep his voice gentle.

"I just have a bad feeling," she murmured.

Gray studied her a moment. He knew all too well what it felt like to have his gut instincts telling him something was wrong. They'd been ambushed during their final mission, unable to protect themselves. The entire area of the desert had been too damn quiet. Too still.

And then all hell had broken loose.

Lena and Kaylee had been ambushed in the hall of the coffee shop. It wasn't the same, yet it was. They hadn't been able to fight their captors, men bigger and stronger than they were. Lena had a knife held to her throat as she'd been hauled away. She'd had her freedom taken from her, her free will.

"It's normal to be afraid after going through an ordeal like that," he said. "It'll take time. And some things you never recover from," he added darkly.

Her eyes shone with tears as she looked at him, and then Gray was moving toward her, muttering a curse under his breath as he set the papers on the table. Lena went to him instantly, her arms gentle as she hugged him. He felt his chest clench. She remembered his scars. "It's okay," he soothed, feeling her soft curves press against him. "We're going to find him. I'll keep you safe."

She sniffled. "I was so scared the other night—until you came," she added, making his heart clench. Gray wasn't normally a soft man, but something about Lena made all his protective instincts roar to life. He wanted to make her feel safe and claim her as his own. Take her to bed and soothe away all those fears, making her forget everything but him.

"I'll come stay over again." It wasn't a question. Gray would do everything in his power to make her feel comfortable in her home. He was already kicking himself for not adding more security cameras. She had the one on her doorbell, but Lena's home and fenced-in yard backed up to a wooded lot. She insisted she was okay, and he of all people should've seen past that.

"I can't ask you to do that."

Gray pulled back, cocking a brow at her. "Why the

hell not? Besides, you didn't ask me. I just offered."

"Because…just because."

His lips quirked. Lena looked so damn cute when she was flustered. Normally, she was pulled together and poised. It made his chest fill with male pride at the way she reacted to him. He affected her. And hell if he didn't love the way she responded to him. Gray brushed back a strand of her silky hair, noting the hint of pink spreading across her cheeks. "That's not a reason," he said, his gaze intense as he looked at her.

Lena's chest rose and fell, her breasts pressing against the silky blouse she wore. Her curves were feminine and gorgeous, and his hands itched to explore all of them. The air seemed to grow thick between them, and he had to force himself to remain in place, to not move in and kiss the hell out of her right now.

"What's happening?" she asked softly.

Gray turned that thought over in his mind, not sure how much he wanted to reveal. "I haven't dated a woman since my Army days," he finally said. "I've been dealing with my own troubles, but I've noticed you, Lena. Ever since I first joined the guys on the team. And while I've kept my distance for a variety of reasons, I'm not sure I can stay away from you anymore."

Her breath hitched, but there was no fear in her eyes. Her cheeks were flushed, her rosy lips parted. His gaze dropped to them briefly, wondering what she tasted like. He wanted to taste her all over, learning her body with his hands and mouth. His tongue. He'd tease and explore her soft skin, feminine curves, and that sweet spot between her parted thighs until she was panting. Breathless. Begging him to make her come.

"I don't want you to stay away."

"Thank God," he murmured. Gray moved slowly so as not to spook her, but then his hands were in her hair, tilting her head back, and his lips were on hers. Lena whimpered and submitted to him, clutching onto his shirt, letting Gray take complete control. Her mouth was soft and so fucking sweet. Her lips parted, and then his tongue was sliding inside. Claiming. He lightly thrust it in and out, foreshadowing exactly what he'd do when they made love.

She pressed even closer to him, her full breasts pillowing against his chest, and Gray was certain she could feel his throbbing erection against her stomach. She made a tiny whimper but didn't pull away, and Gray wanted to roar in approval.

Lena tasted sweet, like strawberries and caramel, and just one quick taste already had him rock hard. She was sexy as hell in her snug, silky blouse and tight skirt, not to mention those heels, but it was more than that. Lena was strong yet innocent somehow, despite the hell she'd been through. Gray hated that she'd endured any of it, but he was so damn thankful she was okay and here in his arms.

He kissed her more deeply, one muscled arm wrapping around her. Lena's hands moved from their grip on the front of his shirt to his biceps. Her nails dug into his skin, and he liked the slight bite of pain. It reminded him he was alive. Gray was a survivor, too.

The beep beep sound of someone typing in the code to the armory had them both stepping back, and a wave of possessiveness washed over him as he took in Lena's flushed cheeks and disheveled appearance.

She was already smoothing her hair and her skirt, but her lips looked swollen from his heated kisses. Gray turned away from the door so no one could see his erection pressing against his pants. Lena's eyes widened in surprise, and then she grabbed the papers they'd set down and stepped in front of him, all business.

"I'll get these numbers to Jett," she said, walking briskly to the door as Ford came in. He looked surprised to see them both inside the armory. Gray glanced back at the boxes on the shelf in front of him. He had no idea what the fuck was inside.

"Am I interrupting something?" Ford asked as Lena disappeared into the hall, the door swinging shut behind her.

Gray removed a box from the shelf, pretending to inspect it. "Nope. We were just finishing up."

"Sure thing, man," Ford said with a chuckle.

Gray muttered a curse.

"You two are good for each other," Ford said. "You both might have your own demons, but that doesn't mean you don't deserve to be happy." Gray glanced over his shoulder again at Ford, studying his teammate. It was a surprisingly insightful thing to say. He and his buddies didn't usually chat about shit like this. "You're happier when she's around. Don't deny it."

"Who's denying it?" Gray asked. He shoved the box back on the shelf and strode to the door, not saying another word as he stalked out of the armory. He didn't blame Lena for rushing off given Ford's sudden arrival, but he needed to make sure she was okay. Gray hadn't planned on kissing her like that, claiming her with his mouth and tongue, but hell. He didn't regret it one bit. And judging from the pretty flush on her face and arousal in her eyes before she'd hurried off, Lena didn't have an issue with it either.

"You got some of Lena's lipstick on you, buddy!" Ford called out.

Gray cursed, listening to his friend's laughter as the door swung shut. They weren't fooling anyone, but he didn't think he gave a shit if the whole world knew. Lena's kidnapping had changed everything. He wasn't content to sit in the shadows watching life go by anymore.

Chapter 8

Lena pushed her shopping cart through the grocery store the next evening, unable to stop a smile from spreading across her face. Gray had found her after their kiss in the armory yesterday. It was sweet that he had checked up on her. She got the feeling Gray wasn't normally like that around women. He was protective of her, and Lena secretly loved that.

She was sure she'd been beet red when she walked past Ford, but he'd married Clara, the receptionist at Shadow Security. It's not like he'd have a problem with anyone dating in the workplace.

Gray had stayed over last night, crashing on her sofa. They'd exchanged a few more heated kisses, but nothing further had happened. She hadn't suggested he stay in her bedroom. Nor had he pushed for it. She'd actually slept soundly knowing he was there but thought she'd heard Gray at one point in the early morning hours.

Her heart ached for him, knowing what he'd gone through. Briefly, she wondered if he'd chosen to stay on the sofa both nights rather than in the guestroom because he had nightmares. He'd mentioned he didn't sleep well but hadn't gone into further detail.

Did he wake up screaming some nights? Fighting against an invisible enemy?

Maybe that should frighten her, but Lena instinctively knew that Gray wouldn't hurt her. Even if she slept at his side, in his arms, she couldn't imagine he'd ever mistake her for his captors. He hadn't said anything about being awake early. They'd had a quick breakfast together before heading into the office, Gray following her in his big SUV. Lena had felt almost shy asking him to come over tonight for dinner when they'd had a quiet moment alone.

"It's a date," he'd teased, those dark eyes glinting with amusement.

"Well—" She cut herself off, flushing. Gray twisted her up in knots sometimes, but in a good way. She felt all her nerve endings alight whenever he was near, her entire body attuned to him.

He'd ducked down for a lingering kiss before she could continue, his mouth on hers magical. "I'd love to come over," he said, his voice husky. "And I'd love to take you out to dinner this weekend."

She smiled and readily agreed, Gray pulling her close. His short beard had rubbed against her cheek as he'd gently kissed her there, and she'd flushed thinking of it on other sensitive areas of her body. Her breasts. Her belly. Her inner thighs.

"I can't wait to see you tonight," he said. The heat of his muscled body seeped into her own. Lena practically wanted to shiver in delight whenever he held her close. Gray was gruffer and more masculine than any of the men she'd dated in the past, but it wasn't a deterrent at all. While she understood his reasons for keeping his distance, especially given that she was closed-off herself, they'd been dancing around their attraction to each other for a year. She wasn't surprised with how quickly things were now moving forward. While she didn't know every detail about his life or past, she knew who he was as a person. She knew the things that mattered. They might have crazy chemistry when they were together, but it also felt like things just clicked into place with him. He gave her butterflies but made her feel safe. Maybe she should be scared after what had happened mere weeks ago, but she knew the man who'd carried her away from that hellish home would never hurt her. He'd literally done the opposite—he'd risked his own life to keep her safe.

Lena's phone buzzed as she moved down the aisle, and she pulled it free from her designer purse, a flush washing over her skin as she saw Gray's name.

"Hi." She paused, phone at her ear, watching the other shoppers move around past her.

"Hi yourself," he said, his deep voice sending a shiver racing down her spine. "I've been stuck in a briefing all afternoon and didn't get a chance to see you before you left."

"I know. I'm picking up some things at the grocery store before I head home," she said. "Is seven still good for dinner?"

"Sure is. I'm just wrapping up some things here first," Gray said.

"No worries if you're running late. Don't forget that I work for Jett, too," she joked.

Gray's laughter filled the line. "Of course I couldn't forget that. I probably wouldn't have ever met you otherwise, so I guess I should thank the boss for hiring me," he joked. Gray cleared his throat. "Jett also reminded me earlier that there's a camera in the armory."

"Oh my gosh," she said, her cheeks warming. "I knew that but totally forgot in the heat of the moment. I cannot believe Jett saw that."

Gray chuckled. "I don't think he watched it, just told West to erase it so you wouldn't be embarrassed. I forgot about the camera in there as well but sure as hell don't regret kissing you."

She lifted her hand to her mouth, remembering the feel of Gray's warm lips moving over her own. The combination of his sensual mouth and prickly beard was somewhat arousing. Exciting. And if anything, after the kiss they'd shared, she'd wanted more.

"Well, as long as Jett teases you and not me, I'm okay with it," she joked, her cheeks still flaming.

She could almost see him smiling. "No problem, baby girl. I'll take one for the team if it means I get to kiss you. See you soon, all right?"

"Okay. See you soon!"

They ended the call, and she felt like she was floating through the rest of the store. Baby girl. Lena was a fully-grown, capable woman, but she rather liked hearing that term of endearment from Gray's deep voice. He was sweeter than she'd ever imagined him to be. Sweet, yet commanding when he wanted if his kisses were any indication. Lena wondered what he'd be like in bed. Gruff and commanding, yes, but she had no doubt he'd know how to please a woman.

She had no trouble letting him take control when the reward would be so sweet.

She was getting ahead of herself though. Lena needed to finish up at the store and get home before Gray arrived. She was always running errands for Jett, and she was efficient then, quickly moving in and out of places with a lengthy to-do list. This evening, however, it was like she couldn't focus. Nervous butterflies filled her stomach at the thought of Gray spending the night again.

She didn't want him to sleep on the sofa tonight. Even if they didn't have sex, she longed to feel him against her, his big body holding her close while she slept. Waking up in his arms sounded like a dream come true. Lena had seen his hungry looks, despite the fact that they'd done no more than kiss so far. She was ready to have his hands and mouth everywhere. Feel the drag of his calloused fingertips over her skin. See the hot look in his eyes as he undressed her.

Lena wanted all of him. Gray would never push if she wasn't ready, but giving herself over to him felt inevitable. They'd been circling around one another for a year, neither admitting the attraction they felt. Both avoiding getting close for their own personal reasons. Lena didn't want to wait any longer for Gray to make her his own.

***

Gray jogged across the parking lot at work, the cold air washing over his skin. He was in short sleeves again, something his teammates ribbed him about sometimes. The crisp, biting air meant freedom though, and there wasn't a damn thing he could fault about that. And right now? He was in a rush because he was headed over to see Lena.

He'd thoroughly kissed her goodnight yesterday before sending her off to bed. While he'd seen the heated looks she gave him, he wanted her to be comfortable before they made love. If she was nervous, he'd give her all the time she needed. Gray was looking forward to taking her to bed, but while sex was one thing, the thought of sleeping at Lena's side gave him pause. What if he awoke from a nightmare? Thrashed out in his sleep and accidentally harmed her?

Muttering a curse, he buried those thoughts down. There was no need to manifest that shit and make it happen. There were nights he slept okay. They were few and far between, but they happened. He wasn't letting those terrorist assholes take one more thing from him. Gray knew there'd be no better feeling than Lena's naked body pressed up to him while they slept, all soft skin and sexy curves. Just thinking about it soothed something inside him. Yes, he wanted to bury himself deep inside her and make her cry out in ecstasy, but he wanted to protect her as well. Keep her safe, even if from her own nightmares.

And shit. How could he deny her that? If she needed him, Gray couldn't crash on the damn sofa forever. He'd have to figure out a way to keep himself in check.

Gray started his SUV, eager anticipation coursing through him. He was planning to swing by the store and pick up some flowers. He knew Lena was often dropping off things at Jett's request—flowers or God knows what else for Anna. He swore he'd heard the boss asking for lingerie for his wife at one point.

Nothing fazed Lena, and he liked that about her. She didn't bat an eyelash at Jett's unusual requests, and it made Gray feel comfortable with her. She wasn't like some women, uptight over every little thing. Maybe she was nervous sometimes, given what she'd been through, but her personality was down-to-Earth.

Gray also loved the idea of surprising her with flowers. She might be used to handling everything on her own, but making her happy was quickly becoming a top priority for him. After googling the closest florist, he headed there first. Gray shook his head, smirking. He wasn't really the type of man to buy a woman flowers, but things were different with Lena. Gray found himself wanting a whole lot he hadn't considered before.

Twenty minutes later, he was ringing Lena's doorbell, and the surprised look on her face didn't disappoint as she took in the colorful, fragrant bouquet. "These are for you," Gray said unnecessarily, watching the way her eyes lit up. A surprising feeling of satisfaction rolled through him. Hell, if he didn't enjoy making Lena smile like this.

"Thank you! They're so gorgeous."

"Not half as gorgeous as you." It wasn't the type of thing Gray usually said, but it was the goddamn truth. Her cheeks were flushed, her eyes sparkling, and her long hair curled around her breasts, drawing his gaze. He'd thought the very first night he came over that she looked like a siren standing in her doorway, and tonight he was just as smitten. Gray was a goner when it came to this woman. He felt like she was the sun, and he was simply orbiting around her, content to bask in her light.

He stepped inside, his duffle bag still slung over

one shoulder, and pulled her in for a searing kiss. The fact that this was their first date of sorts wasn't lost on him, with Lena inviting him for dinner, yet here he was arriving with flowers and an overnight bag. He couldn't deny it felt right.

Lena was still holding the flowers as Gray took control of their kiss, positioning her head as he wanted. Her face felt small and delicate in his big hands, and Gray wanted to simply devour her. She let out a soft sigh as her lips parted for him, and then his tongue slid inside. Teasing. Claiming. She tasted as sweet as yesterday, and her little whimpers were driving him wild. The scent of her exotic perfume teased his nostrils, and he had to resist breaking off the kiss and burying his nose in her neck, inhaling her intoxicating scent. His cock was already swelling, pressing against his boxers. They'd barely gotten inside the front door, and he wanted her. Badly.

Her lips were swollen when he finally broke off their kiss. "Wow."

He chuckled. "It didn't seem appropriate to kiss you like that at the office earlier."

"Probably not," she said lightly, flashing him a teasing smile. "Come on in."

"You look great," he told her.

He slung his duffle bag down in the living room, setting it by the sofa. "Um," she looked adorably flustered for a moment.

"I'll just leave it there for now," he assured her. "Wherever you want me tonight is good with me." She swallowed and nodded. "Don't be nervous," he said, moving toward her again. "After all, I've been in your bedroom before," he teased.

She flushed, and Gray let his eyes rake over her.

Lena had changed from what she'd worn earlier today at work into a sexy wrap-style dress. Maybe it wasn't meant to be overly revealing, but it perfectly hugged her breasts and displayed a nice amount of cleavage. He'd never seen her wear it at the office, and for that, he was thankful. Lena had killer curves, and he didn't want the other men ogling her. Lena was his, even if she didn't realize it yet.

The sudden thought was as startling as it was right.

"I'm sorry about freaking out last weekend," she said, briefly covering her face with her hands. "I'm still embarrassed you rushed over in the middle of the night."

He took her fluttering hands in his own, laying the flowers on her coffee table. Her hands looked tiny compared to his own muscular ones. Lena was staring at them, too, and he ran a thumb over her knuckles. Her skin was so damn soft. Gray had a feeling she was that silky smooth everywhere. "I was already awake before I came over the other night," he reminded her. "I don't mind coming by if you're scared."

She nodded, a look of uncertainty still crossing her features.

"Lena, I carried you out of that house weeks ago," he said, his voice thick with emotion. "I saw that they'd drugged you. I wanted to rip that guy to shreds, but my only priority was making sure you were okay. We got to the hospital as quickly as we could. If you need me at night because you're frightened, you don't need to ask twice." He cleared his throat, growing more serious. "I feel like I should warn you that I've got demons of my own though. Nightmares. Sometimes I wake up thrashing around and—"

She squeezed his hands. "I know you wouldn't hurt me."

"Maybe, maybe not. I'd never intentionally harm you, but—"

"You wouldn't," she insisted. "I know you could never hurt me. I don't know who those evil men were who captured you, but I'm positive you wouldn't mistake me for them."

"I can't guarantee it," he said, feeling pained. "I might have to hold you until you fall asleep and then crash on the sofa. At least until I'm sure it'd be okay." He didn't miss the way her face fell, and then Gray was brushing back some of her dark hair. "I haven't been with a woman in…a while. Even then, I didn't stay the night."

She bit her lip, suddenly looking worried again.

"Just know if I end up on your sofa, it's not because of you, baby girl. I didn't up and leave, just wanted to keep you safe. I'd rather hold you close all night." Her gaze softened slightly, and Gray leaned down for another kiss. It was gentler than when he'd first come inside but still made his heart pound. She melted against him, her body relaxing into his own, and Gray couldn't resist brushing some of her silky hair back, his lips moving to her neck. Lingering.

"I want to feel you beside me. Feel your body pressed up against mine."

"Gray," she murmured.

He skimmed one hand up her side, his thumb barely brushing against the soft curve of her breast. Hell, she was gorgeous. Lena looked like a delicious present he couldn't wait to unwrap. It was all he could do to not take her to bed right now. Forget dinner.

He would feast on his woman instead. "I want to know what it feels like inside you, to feel you writhing beneath me as you come." Gray's lips brushed over her neck again, and her pulse jumped. "Fuck, you're beautiful," he practically growled.

The oven timer began buzzing, and she jolted in surprise, clinging to him for a moment. It made him feel good to know she trusted him to keep her safe, but he hated that she'd been so easily startled. Lena was already pulling away to hurry to the kitchen, but Gray gently tugged on her hand. He brought it to his mouth, pressing his lips against her knuckles. Lena was breathing heavily, her breasts rising up and down.

Gray guided her to the kitchen. It was like he couldn't keep away. Gray's hands were still on her, one clutching her hand, the other at her waist. Her hips swayed as they walked, and his gaze dropped to the curve of her ass. She was wearing heels again, and he had the brief flash of an idea of seeing her in those and nothing else. The food smelled delicious, completely mouthwatering, but it in no way compared to the woman he wanted to feast on later.

Chapter 9

Lena beamed as they finished dessert—a delicious homemade Crème Brulée. Gray had been shocked when she'd produced the tiny torch to crystalize the sugar. They'd turned out perfectly though—rich and creamy inside with a crisp, decadent top.

"Tell me you didn't use to make these for Jett every week," Gray said with a chuckle.

Lena burst into laughter. "Of course not. I used to prepare many of his meals in advance, but unless Jett was hosting a large gathering, it wasn't anything fancy. Besides, I'm mostly running errands and doing tasks around the office ever since Anna came into the picture."

Gray nodded, rubbing a hand over his short beard. "That makes sense. I know that you and Anna have become friends, but I can surmise that she wouldn't want another woman hovering around all the time."

"Definitely not," Lena agreed. "I helped out with

dinners when Brody was born, but she and Jett generally manage meals on their own now." Lena shrugged. "Things have changed. When Jett first formed Shadow Security, it was a group of single guys—including him. I still do some shopping for him, but he's got a wife now. Life moves on."

"Don't I know it," Gray agreed, his lips quirking. His gaze fell on the flowers. She'd sent him back to the living room for the forgotten bouquet while she'd been plating the food. The colorful arrangement looked pretty in the glass vase she'd put them in. Their eyes met, and for some reason, Lena found herself blushing. Gray was an intense guy. While dinner with him had been easy, the two of them talking as they ate, she hadn't missed his heated looks or occasional light caress.

He was into her, and that was flattering as anything. Gray had seen Lena at her worst, completely drugged and out of it. He never made her feel lesser for being unable to protect herself or escape. Her gaze trailed over him, taking in the veins on his forearms and muscular hands. The bulk of his biceps. Breadth of his shoulders. He was good looking enough that he could easily get any woman he wanted. Yet he was here. With her.

Gray licked his lips, rising to clear the table. She smoothed her hands over her thighs, suddenly feeling nervous. Gray caught her around the waist after she'd set her wineglass in the sink, moving to cage her in against the counter. His big hand brushed back her hair, and she felt a flurry of shivers washing over her. One simple touch from him made her heartbeat increase, but she loved the way he couldn't seem to keep his hands off her. Gray both made her feel safe and made her heart race.

"Dinner was incredible." His dark eyes were intense as he looked down at her, his full lips looking positively kissable. He smelled faintly of pine again, mixed in with the clean, masculine scent that was pure Gray.

"I'm glad you enjoyed it," she said, lightly running her hands up his chest. She could feel his firm muscles beneath, the heat radiating off his bulky frame. He was wearing short sleeves yet again, and she could see the hint of his tattoo peeking out beneath one sleeve. "This is okay, right?" she asked, suddenly realizing her hands on his chest might bother him.

He looked surprised for a beat then relaxed. "Oh. Yeah. I have scars on my back, but my chest doesn't ever bother me. I did have a few broken ribs, but those have long since healed." Lena's mouth dropped open, surprise washing over her. He said it so casually, she almost wondered if she'd misheard. He'd been beaten. Hurt. "Hey," he said huskily, lightly dragging his knuckles over one cheek. "I'm okay. It was hell at the time, and like I said, I have nightmares. You won't hurt me, Lena."

Tears filled her eyes, and Gray's gaze softened. "I promise it's okay," he assured her. "I love your hands on me."

She giggled, suddenly feeling foolish, and a stray tear spilled over, running down her cheek. Gray gently thumbed it away, and she closed her eyes, trying to keep her emotions in check. She felt Gray lean closer, and then he was softly kissing one eyelid, then the other. Lena's breath caught. She opened her eyes and stared into his, trying to read all the emotions dancing within them. Tenderness. Affection. Arousal, too, his pupils widening as they both became aware of their bodies pressed together. She could feel the bulge in his jeans, Gray already hot and hard for her.

Gray was pure male. More gruff and masculine than any guy she'd dated before, but she was drawn to him in a way she couldn't explain.

Unable to stop herself, Lena rose to her tiptoes and kissed him. It was the first time she'd taken the lead, but Gray let her have control for the moment. His hands were gentle as he held her, and Lena kissed him deeper, her hands moving to his short-cropped hair. His beard rubbed against her sensitive skin, and she slid her tongue inside his mouth, exploring. When she pressed her body even closer to him, Gray growled, lifting her atop the counter. She gasped in surprise, but then his mouth was on hers again, hot and hungry.

Shamelessly, she spread her legs, letting him edge even closer between her thighs. One big hand cupped her neck, his thumb sliding over her throat as he took control of their kiss. She whimpered as he claimed her mouth, and then his hand was trailing lower, skimming over her cleavage, cupping one breast through her dress. She arched against him, moaning. Gray was big everywhere. His hands. His muscles. His cock as he pressed against her core.

He squeezed her breast gently, his thumb toying with her nipple through the material of her dress and bra. Arousal dampened her folds, and suddenly, she wanted to feel Gray everywhere.

"Take me to bed," she told him between kisses, the heat rising between them.

"Are you sure?" he asked, pinning her with his dark gaze.

She bit her lip and nodded, Gray's eyes shifting to her mouth. He slid his thumb over her lower lip, breathing heavily. As her gaze dropped to the impressive bulge in his pants, she could see the tension in his muscles, the way he was holding back. Her eyes once again slid to meet his. "You're so fucking pretty, Lena." And then he lifted her in his arms as if she weighed nothing, striding down the hall like he'd done it every night. She flipped on the light switch as they entered her bedroom, and Gray set her down, Lena wobbling slightly in her heels. They were instantly all over each other again, kissing, touching, Gray backing her toward the bed.

***

Gray's cock pressed against his boxers as he unwrapped Lena's dress between kisses. She'd tugged his shirt off when they'd gotten into her bedroom but still hadn't seen his back. His scars. He was too far gone to worry about that now. Lena looked like a goddess, all swollen lips and tousled hair, gorgeous curves, and breasts that rose and fell with every breath. She had on a sexy black bra, satin and lace that perfectly hugged her full breasts. Her creamy cleavage was mouthwatering on display like that, and he couldn't resist reaching out, skimming his fingers over her soft skin.

Her dress fell to the floor with a final tug of the tie, and his dick twitched. Lena in her lacy bra, matching black thong, and sky-high heels was a sight to behold. He was moving before he thought about it.

His big hands gripped her hips, and then he was lying her down on the bed, coming down atop her, his forearms resting on either side of her head. Lena's arms wrapped around his neck. Gray could feel the heat of her core, and ran one hand down her side, cupping a bare ass cheek and giving her a squeeze. Her legs came up and around him, her heels digging into him, and Gray resisted the urge to groan.

Lena was an absolute vixen, sexy without even realizing it. Everything she did notched up his arousal another level. He nuzzled against her cheek for a moment, trying to keep himself in check, to make it good for her, and then his hands and mouth were everywhere.

Gray kissed his way across her cleavage, tugging one cup of her bra down. A rosy nipple drew his gaze, and he kissed it, listening to her short gasp before he began licking the pebbled bud. Sucking. Listening to Lena's pleas for more. Her short nails dug into his scalp, and he smiled. His girl was sensitive. Gray could spend hours feasting on her breasts, but then he'd miss out on the main course.

He wanted nothing more than to thrust into her silken walls, letting her cries of pleasure fill the bedroom.

Gray lightly bit down on Lena's taut bud, listening to her small moan. He blew gently on her nipple, soothing the sting, and felt satisfaction roil through him as she bucked beneath him. She was eager, and her responses gave him a thrill. Moving to her other breast, he tugged down that cup as well, her lacy bra now pushing both breasts up toward him like an offering. He kissed and laved at her other pink nipple, Lena squirming below him. Gray reached beneath her, unfastening the pretty bra, and watched in satisfaction as both breasts spilled free. He tossed the lacy lingerie to the floor, ready to simply devour her.

She lay topless on her bed, wearing nothing but a thong and those come-fuck-me heels. Both of Lena's nipples were hard, a pretty pink against her fair skin. It was a sight he'd never forget, Lena flushed and vulnerable, nearly naked, trusting him to give her what she needed. "You're gorgeous," he said huskily, kissing both breasts again. Squeezing. Playfully nipping. "So damn gorgeous."

Lena's hands moved to his shoulders, clinging to him, and he tried not to wince as she accidentally brushed over a scar near his shoulder blades. She'd discover them soon enough. In the meantime, he liked that she was already too far gone from his attention to think about them. Gray needed to taste her. See her pretty pussy. Hear her crying out his name.

Gray nuzzled against her breasts, knowing the scruff of his beard was teasing her sensitive skin. He kissed his way down to her stomach, slow and intentional. Lena sucked in a breath as he reached the triangle of fabric covering her pussy. Gray kissed her lower lips through the material, the sweet scent of her arousal teasing his nostrils. She was already soaked, so ready for him. He rubbed her clit through the satin material with his thumb, a wet spot already forming. "I bet you taste amazing," he murmured. "Is this all for me, baby girl?"

"Yes," she breathed, unable to hold back a moan as he slid his thumb over her swollen bud again.

Meeting her gaze, he shifted forward, lightly nipping at her hip. His teeth caught the edge of her thong, and her eyes widened as he began to tug it down with his mouth. She lifted her hips, urging him on, and then he was gripping her skimpy thong in his hands, dragging it down her legs.

Gray froze as he looked back at her. Lena's pussy was bare, glistening with her arousal. He ran his hands up her smooth legs, leaving her thong around her ankles. For the briefest flash of a moment, he wondered if that would bother her, give her a feeling of being tied down and trapped in a bed again. But there was nothing but arousal in her eyes. He eased her legs over his shoulders, Lena held in place by both Gray's body and the tiny scrap of fabric at her slender ankles. His mouth hovered over her sex, his hands wrapping around her hips. Lena's breasts rose and fell as she panted, both of them hanging in the moment. Gray met her eyes, and as Lena watched him, leaned in and put his mouth on her feminine flesh.

Chapter 10

Lena gasped as Gray kissed her pussy, his full lips and rough beard on her most tender flesh. He pressed his lips to her slowly, teasing her, seeming to enjoy her reactions. His hot gaze pinned her in place even more than his big body ever could, and as she watched him, panting, pleading for more, he began to devour her. She writhed helplessly against Gray's face as he licked her swollen folds, her arousal coating his short beard.

She mumbled incoherently, her pleasure already spiking higher. Gray knew exactly what he was doing. Each teasing lick and long swipe of his tongue was meant to drive her wild. His broad shoulders spread her thighs apart, and she couldn't pull away with her thong stretched around her spread ankles. Nor did she want to.

Gray's big hands moved to her breasts, squeezing and kneading, and as he pinched both nipples, she cried out. He growled and gave a long, hard lick up her slit, teasing every sensitive fold. Gray sucked her clit between his full lips as she cried out at the sensation, then began to work her with his tongue. White hot pleasure shot through her, Lena's entire existence suddenly consisting of Gray's masterful mouth. He didn't let up as she expected, just drove her higher and higher.

The scruff of his beard rubbed against her sensitive, swollen flesh, adding another layer to her pleasure. His thumbs rubbed over her nipples again, the sensation shooting straight to her core. Need roiled through her, her inner walls clamping down around nothing. Gray's tongue flicked faster over her sensitive bud, Lena gasping out his name. His mouth was making love to her pussy, and she couldn't hold back any more. Gray lightly grazed his teeth over her swollen clit, and she screamed, the unexpected sensation pushing her over the edge.

Lena's legs shook on his wide shoulders, and Gray eased her down from her orgasmic high, softly kissing her fluttering folds.

Lena was gasping. Breathless.

The man hadn't even been inside of her yet, and she'd come harder than ever before. As she lay there panting, she realized she should've been frightened. The man who'd kidnapped her had tied her to his bed. Threatened vile things.

She felt nothing but safe and overflowing with emotion here with Gray.

He shifted, kissing her stomach, then settled between her legs again and stayed there, a satisfied look on his face as he gave her another lazy swipe of his tongue.

She blushed, taking in his pleased expression. Gray

knew exactly what he was doing, keeping her legs spread wide, exposing her sex to his heated gaze. "You're going to come for me again, baby girl."

He licked her swollen folds, lingering. Savoring her taste. And then he was pushing his tongue inside her molten channel, his beard rough against her arousal drenched skin. His hands shifted, sliding down to her ass as he tilted her hips slightly upward, and then he began to thrust his tongue in and out of her pussy, fucking her with his mouth.

She moaned, actually moaned for this man. Every nerve ending was firing, Lena already oversensitive from her first orgasm. She was bare and exposed, unable to move away from Gray's sensual assault and not sure she'd ever want to. As the heat grew within her belly, coiling down, she bucked up against his mouth.

Gray growled, and she felt the low rumble against her sex. He shifted one hand, his thumb circling her clit as she cried out. Gray's tongue was masterful, moving in and out, and with her inner walls beginning to spasm around him, she screamed, fisting the sheets with both hands as she came and came.

Lena was limp with pleasure, unable to move, as Gray gently lowered her legs from his big shoulders. Lena's heels fell off, and he pulled the thong free of her ankles. Briefly, she got a glimpse of his back, of white scars against his flesh, but he was already crawling up beside her and rolling them over, tugging up the covers. She wanted to protest, to reciprocate, to explore Gray's muscles and ridges, but she was already falling asleep against him.

She felt his lips press against her temple, his arms tightening around her. Lena was thoroughly sated, and as she drifted off, knew she'd never want another man again.

Chapter 11

Gray crossed the conference room two days later, frowning at the data West was passing out to the team. "Ivan Rogers most frequently travels to Cancun, Mexico and San Diego, California aboard private planes," West said. "Note the number of flights to each location. He's been to Miami multiple times, but it hardly compares to his top two destinations. While Rogers does have a home in San Diego, he's there more frequently than any of his other properties."

"Do you think he's crossing the border?" Ford asked.

"Damn straight he is," Jett said, his gaze narrowing as he looked at the number of flights. "He's got multiple connections in Mexico. It's not just American women that have been caught up and sold in his sex-trafficking ring. He travels where the women and buyers are. As we all know, there are many men who've made lucrative profits off of selling innocent women. There are just as many men willing to pay a hefty sum for a female."

The team exchanged a glance. Luke's girlfriend Wren had met him while searching for her own sister in Mexico. Ivan Rogers was hardly the first sick bastard they'd gone after.

"Do we know when he last went to San Diego?" Luke asked. "This data compiles the number of flights but doesn't show the dates when each occurred."

"Three weeks ago," West confirmed, crossing to his laptop. He typed in something, and then the travel dates and locations appeared on the big screen. "Here's the kicker. While I have flight data of where he's been traveling for several years, there's been nothing for weeks. Not a single damn flight booked by Rogers. Somehow, he showed up in New York, but it wasn't aboard a private plane."

"Unless he was using an alias," Gray pointed out.

"While possible, his cease of travel via private jets started prior to the kidnapping," West explained. "The Feds hadn't raided his homes yet. He'd have no reason to think he was being watched any more than usual."

"Something changed," Sam said with a frown.

"Yes, but we don't know what," West agreed. "For whatever reason, Rogers stopped booking private flights before the women were kidnapped here in New York."

"Did he assume he was being tracked?" Nick asked with a frown. "We know he wasn't being tracked via his private flights at that time, but maybe he thought someone was onto him. Cronin and

Levins had taken Kaylee to the safehouse by then. They were hired by the military officer at Offutt, but Rogers could've been involved somehow and we missed it."

"It doesn't add up," Gray said. "It's like he suspected he was being watched and suddenly stopped booking any and all private flights."

"Maybe he had a falling out with the company or a pilot," Ford said.

Jett drummed his fingers on the table. "Maybe he was planning an escape. Those goons working for him on other jobs were no doubt raising suspicions by taking Kaylee. Her disappearance from Offutt wouldn't have gone unnoticed. Even if Rogers wasn't directly involved in that escapade, maybe he decided to get out."

"And go where?" Gray pressed. "Mexico?"

"Lena said he was going to keep her," Nick said, his voice eerily calm.

"He didn't know Lena before the kidnapping," Gray said, feeling his blood pressure rise at the thought of Lena with that monster. "If she hadn't been with Kaylee, she never would've been kidnapped."

"Maybe he wanted Kaylee," Nick said, his voice growing hard. "Those assholes Cronin and Levins were filming her at the safehouse. Say Rogers saw the footage and decided he needed her—either for himself or his sex-trafficking operation. For whatever reason, he saw Lena when they kidnapped both of them, and fixated on her instead."

"He's a sick fuck," Gray muttered.

West's gaze was moving between the men. "The problem is we don't know his current location. I retrieved the flight records and can go back through his travel for years. He's constantly on the move, and I know every single time he's hired a private jet. If we'd gotten this data mere weeks ago, we could've determined his probable location. Narrowed down the places he was selling girls. Brought him in. The trouble is, he hasn't gotten on an airplane in weeks."

"The Feds didn't mention any fake identification when they raided his home," Luke pointed out. "If he's traveling under an alias, he'd have to be carrying it on his person."

"He's an arrogant prick," Jett said, his eyes hard. "He thought he could get away with traveling under his own name because nothing stuck until now. The Feds tried arresting him before but he was out on bond within hours."

"How the hell is that even possible?" Ford asked.

Jett eyed him. "Money talks. He had his lackeys do the dirty work and managed to keep himself clean. Until Lena and Kaylee."

"The FBI profiler has an entire dossier on him," West said. "Ivan Rogers is narcissistic and arrogant. He's driven by sex and money. Obsessive. Maybe he fixated on Kaylee, enjoying the footage his men shared with him from the safehouse, and wanted to keep her. Either way, that changed when he saw Lena. It'll be harder to travel now with the Feds looking for him, knowing he's wanted for kidnapping and assault. He's going to take what he wants and flee."

"And what he wants is Lena," Gray said, horror washing over him.

"You think he's still in New York," Jett said, crossing his arms. "You think he's still out there, waiting."

West nodded, his voice grim. "I think he'll come back for Lena."

***

Gray mumbled and thrashed around, trying to escape from the ropes that bound him in place. A fine sheen of sweat coated his skin, his heart racing. His fists clenched in anger and frustration, and he sucked in a breath, the dry desert air doing nothing to quench his thirst. He tried to shout out a warning but couldn't speak. Couldn't find his voice.

He couldn't stop them.

Couldn't help her.

Gray couldn't move, no matter how hard he tried.

"Lena. Lena!"

He gasped as he awoke, taking shaky breaths. He was tense and agitated, twisted in the sheets. The darkness and cool air surprised him. It wasn't blindingly bright or stifling hot like the desert. He wasn't in that fucking tent.

Gray sucked in another breath, trying to get his bearings as he sat up in bed, his body shaking.

"Shhh, it's okay," a sweet, feminine voice murmured, soft hands running down his arm. Soothing. Comforting. A woman's gentle touch. Surprisingly, he began to calm down, his body instinctively knowing he was safe.

Gray looked over in the darkness, awareness suddenly washing over him. "Lena?" he croaked.

"I'm right here, baby. You had another nightmare."

One hand slid to his nape, lightly applying pressure. It was grounding. It reminded him he was in bed with his girl, not tied up in Afghanistan.

"Another one?" he asked, his voice low.

"You were murmuring and restless earlier but didn't wake up. This one seemed worse."

"Shit." His head fell to his hands, a feeling of defeat washing over him. He'd slept soundly the past few nights at Lena's side, in her bed, but the briefing earlier today with Jett and his teammates had rattled him. Gray hadn't been in fear of his own pain, of the evil men who'd gleefully hurt him, of the torture he'd endured. He'd been fucking terrified because Lena needed him, and he couldn't save her.

Her soft hands kept running over his bare arms and shoulders, her touch light and gentle. It was a welcome relief. She paused, clearly feeling the scars on his back as she gave him a careful hug. While he'd undressed Lena and pleasured her every night, he'd been careful to make it about her enjoyment. He hadn't let her explore his own scarred body. He hadn't made love to her yet either, wanting to make sure it felt right.

She softly kissed his bare shoulder, and Gray's arms came around her, holding her close. Her soft skin, bare breasts, and warmth felt like fucking heaven. Gray's heart thundered in his chest. He felt safe in the dark here with her. He might be stronger than her physically, able to protect her from harm, but mentally? She was the one shielding him from his nightmares.

Hell if he didn't need her as much as she needed him.

"Did you dream you were back in Afghanistan?" Lena asked softly, pulling back to look at him. The covers had slipped down, and he could see her perfect breasts in the moonlight. Fuck, she was beautiful. Long, dark hair. Fair skin. Gorgeous curves. Her breasts hung heavy and full, her nipples peaked. He'd explored every inch of her earlier, Lena collapsing in a satisfied heap atop him shortly after. She'd wanted to touch him, but he'd made her come twice, making sure she was thoroughly sated. She'd been too exhausted to do more than fall asleep in his arms.

Now he was wide awake in the middle of the night, tormented by dreams that weren't even real.

He huffed out a sigh. "This was different. Usually, I have nightmares about my captors. My torture. I dream that I'm tied up in that goddamn tent, bleeding and in pain."

"And this time?" she asked quietly when he didn't continue.

Gray looked up, meeting her worried eyes in the shadows. He couldn't see her too well in the moonlight, but he knew without a doubt she hurt for him. She'd shed tears on his behalf before, when she was worried she'd hurt him. It had felt like his own heart was being ripped out, seeing her upset. Lena was sweet as honey, empathetic to his pain, and nothing but light and goodness. While he felt like he shouldn't touch her with his own darkness, the moment felt quiet and safe. "This time I was upset because I couldn't save you." His voice sounded thick. Tortured. If Lena was ever hurt because he couldn't get to her, Gray didn't know what he'd do.

He didn't miss her quiet intake of breath. Just as quickly, she was soothing him once more, pulling

Gray close. He let her lay them back down, Gray's head pillowed on her bare breasts. It was both intimate and comforting. "I'm okay," she soothed, her hands running over his head. "I'm right here." His breathing was still ragged, but Lena was so warm and reassuring and real. He was safe from his nightmares in her arms. But when he fell asleep again?

Gray tensed.

"What are you thinking?" she asked, stroking her slender fingers over his head once more.

"I'm just worried about falling asleep and having another nightmare. I could've hurt you thrashing around like that," he admitted. Her breasts rose and fell beneath his cheek, and Gray's hand slid to her hip, cupping it possessively. He was only partly lying on Lena so as not to crush her, but he wanted to mark every part of her as his. Kiss her all over. Mark her with his scent. Fill her with his seed.

It was a startling thought. He didn't think he wanted kids, but he wasn't opposed to seeing Lena pregnant with their child. Gray was jumping way ahead of himself, however. They hadn't even had sex yet, and when they did, he'd certainly wear a condom.

But Lena, pregnant with his baby, filled him with a possessiveness that shocked him.

"You'd never hurt me," she said vehemently. "You told me yourself the nightmare was because you couldn't get to me. Even in your sleep, your subconscious wants to keep me safe."

Her hands shifted, lighting running over his back. Gray realized she could probably see his scars in the moonlight. He'd stripped his shirt off every night, knowing she could see him if she wanted, but he hadn't given Lena a chance to explore his body. He'd been too busy ravishing her to worry about himself. Tasting her everywhere. Making her come on his fingers, mouth, and tongue.

Her fingertips trailed carefully over the scars near his shoulder blades, her touch whisper light. "I hate them for hurting you," she passionately said.

Gray closed his eyes, his head pillowed by her breasts, his mind whirling. He didn't want to think about those fuckers. He wanted Lena. All of her. His grip at her hip tightened. Turning his head, he kissed her plump breast, shifting up to pull her nipple into his mouth. She gasped out loud but didn't shift away, and then Gray was moving. Touching her soft skin with his calloused hands. Kissing and caressing her everywhere. Her legs parted as he buried his face between her thighs, and before long, Lena's sweet cries were filling the bedroom.

"Make love to me," she pleaded as he kissed his way up her stomach afterward, her sweet taste still on his tongue. Gray wasn't sure he could hold back anymore. He kissed his way across her breasts, rubbing his beard over her skin, then hovered above her body. Lingered. He stared down into her dark eyes, his biceps bunching as he held his weight, then kissed her, hard.

Lena's arms and legs wrapped around him, pulling him down to her. Holding him close.

"Condom," he muttered.

Lena licked her lips as Gray rose and crossed toward his bag, his dick already rock hard against his boxers. He grabbed the box of condoms he'd tossed in his duffle, carrying it over. Lena was stretched out on the bed in the moonlight, her creamy skin and womanly curves on display. She was beautiful. Full breasts. Pert nipples. Bare pussy. And long, satiny legs he couldn't wait to feel wrapped around him as he finally claimed her as his own.

Lena surprised him by sitting up and scooting over to the edge of the bed, her breasts bouncing with the movement. As Gray watched, she pulled him closer, her hands holding his waist, her mouth right at his erection. Lena gripped his thick length through the soft cotton, her thumb rubbing over his engorged head. His dick twitched, but Gray otherwise held still, barely daring to move. The sound of his heavy breathing filled the bedroom, and his entire body was tense, ready to snap.

Lena tugged his boxers down, not hesitating in the slightest, and Gray dropped the box of condoms as her hot, wet mouth wrapped around him. She didn't just put his head between her lips, she sucked him deep, her hand gripping the base of his shaft.

Gray choked out a cry, her mouth and tongue the most incredible thing he'd ever felt. Gray had been with other women over the years, but nothing compared to Lena's mouth wrapped around his cock, those dark eyes looking up at him as she sucked him off.

Lena eagerly bobbed her head on his shaft, her free hand moving to cup his balls. Gray felt them tightening, his pending eruption bearing down on him. His hands slid through her hair, his fingers tightening on her silky strands, and he gently eased her off his erection, his chest heaving. "I want to come inside you," he said, his voice strained.

She nodded, her lips swollen, then scooted back on the bed, resting on her elbows to watch him. Her long hair curled around her breasts enticingly, her gaze raking over him. Gray retrieved the condoms and sheathed himself as her legs parted. He was barely hanging on as it was, nearly ready to explode, and Lena was lying there offering herself to him like the best fucking present he'd ever received.

He paused for a moment, drinking her in. Lena's dark eyes were on him, the moment soft despite the passion raging through his bloodstream. It felt like everything would change after this. Lena would be his, body and soul.

Gray prowled over her, his erection jutting out in front of him. He was hard as steel, on edge and ready for his woman. His cock slid through her folds as he kissed her, Lena falling back on the bed once more. Her fingers eagerly raked through his short hair, her legs coming up around him. Gray notched himself at her entrance, throbbing, and then pushed inside the tightest, hottest pussy he'd ever felt.

Lena gasped at his penetration and clung to Gray, her body trying to take all of him. Gray was big. Everywhere. And Lena was so fucking tight. She felt like a dream. He continued to ease in slowly, holding himself back until she got used to his size and possession of her. Gray kissed her again, soothing, teasing, and felt Lena begin to relax around him. Testing her readiness, he gently thrust, her slickened walls easing his way. Lena moaned as he bottomed out inside her, and he grunted, trying to keep himself from erupting right then and there.

"You're big," she panted, her cheeks flushed and eyes wide.

He kissed her again, thrusting in time with his next words. "You're tight. Hot. Perfect."

Lena keened, arching against him as the base of his shaft rubbed against her swollen clit. "Gray," she moaned as he rubbed against her again. "Gray. Oh my God."

"I've got you, baby girl."

Twining her slender fingers with his own, he lifted her arms above her head, pinning her hands to the bed. She clung to him almost desperately, crying out again as he increased the speed of his thrusts. Lena's inner walls were already spasming around him, still swollen and ready from her earlier orgasm. She tightened her legs around his waist, and as Gray thrust harder, faster, Lena screamed out his name, her pussy gripping him tightly.

Gray felt her fluttering around him, squeezing his cock as she orgasmed, and then he was coming, too, hot seed filling the condom. He mumbled her name, shocked at the intensity of their joining. He'd always been able to keep in control before, to hold off and come when he was ready, but Lena's own orgasm had sent him over the edge.

He huffed out another breath above her, trying to hold himself up so he didn't crush her. Lena was flushed and gorgeous, panting, and looking like the prettiest damn thing he'd ever seen. Gray rolled them both over, too sated to even care as the sheets rubbed against his back. Lena had been wrapped around him, too, and he'd barely noticed any discomfort. It was hard to even remember his scars as aftershocks of pleasure rocked through him, his body drowsy and sated.

Lena was draped over him, Gray's cock still half-hard inside her. He needed to deal with the condom, to get up, but his body was too slack to even move at the moment.

"Oh my God," she murmured quietly.

He turned his head, pressing his lips to her temple. Gray's arms tightened around her, holding her closer still. "Thank you," he said, his voice rough with emotion.

She nuzzled against him for a moment, kissing his jaw. His mouth. "For what?" she asked, her voice soft and drowsy as she gazed down at him. Lena looked content and satisfied. A woman thoroughly pleasured. But it was the easy comfort he felt with her that made him feel safe.

He kissed her roughly, stealing her breath.

"For bringing me back to life."

Chapter 12

Lena glanced over her shoulder a few days later, unable to shake the feeling that she was being watched. She shifted the bags of groceries in her arms, moving more quickly across the parking lot toward her vehicle.

The past several nights had been amazing—a whirlwind of sex, sleep, and repeat. Gray had taken to staying over at her house every day, their easy dinners and conversation after work followed with nights of lovemaking. She was shocked at how easily Gray always got her body to respond to him, but she was also loving the feeling of being in Gray's arms. Of him thrusting inside her, filling her in a way that made her heart want to explode right along with the rest of her senses.

Just thinking about all the ways that Gray made her come had her blushing. And while she loved sleeping beside him, she knew there was another reason he wanted to be there at her home.

Ivan Rogers.

Gray had informed her that the sex-trafficking ring kingpin was missing. Vanished. Gone without a trace. While he typically jetted off on private flights, staying at his many properties and conducting his dirty business dealings at nearby locations, the man was simply gone. Her kidnapping weeks ago had changed things. She knew that. Ivan Rogers had been directly involved with Lena and Kaylee's abduction. With that development, including Rogers literally driving the getaway vehicle and drugging Lena himself before trying to assault her, the Feds had moved in. Raided his homes. Seized his computers and files. Frozen his bank accounts.

But Ivan was nowhere to be found.

She'd discussed the situation with Jett and Gray multiple times already, unease washing over her. While she'd surmised that Ivan Rogers had simply traveled under a false identity, making him untraceable, Jett didn't think that was the case. No falsified documents had been found at his homes. No records of flights booked under aliases had been documented in the papers they'd unearthed. He'd prided himself on being one step ahead of the law, and that included traveling under his own name, knowing that he'd been untouchable.

Jett believed he was still in New York. Ivan had come here for a reason, inserting himself directly in Kaylee's kidnapping and wanting a piece of the action.

Except Lena had been there, too. Taken. Held hostage. Hurt.

And Ivan had sworn that he'd never let her go.

Inexplicably, she shivered, looking around once more. The empty cars near her car felt almost ominous. Threatening. There were people around the parking lot, rushing to and from the store on the way home from work, but if someone jumped out at her, could she really be saved? Her car felt almost secluded at the end of the aisle, and she was eager to get out of there.

Lena popped the trunk of her car, setting the bags of groceries inside. Her fingers slid into her coat pocket, clutching her car keys. She had a new canister of pepper spray attached to her keychain. Gray had offered to train her in firing a weapon. Lena didn't want a gun though, knowing it would most likely be used against her. She didn't have any of Gray's training, expertise, or strength. She'd be cautious but otherwise had to live her life.

Steeling herself, she scanned the parking lot again. No one would jump out at her. There were cameras. Witnesses. And Gray would've told her if simply running errands was unsafe. Still feeling uneasy, she shut the trunk and then climbed into her vehicle. Lena had groceries to deliver and other tasks to get done before Gray came over tonight.

Twenty minutes later, Lena pulled up to the gate of Jett and Anna's large home, the transponder in her vehicle allowing the large wrought iron barrier to slide open. She'd picked up some things at the grocery store for them since Anna hadn't been feeling well and Jett had been in briefings all afternoon. Pulling up the long driveway of the tree-lined property, her gaze swept over the area out of habit.

The sun had nearly dipped below the horizon, and the winter chill in the air made her shiver. Even bundled up and inside of her vehicle, it felt like she couldn't get warm. It had been a long week, and something about the evening just felt ominous.

A lone car passed on the secluded road, driving right by the house. She watched it go from her own vehicle, knowing Jett had cameras everywhere. Lena pulled up and parked outside of the big garage just as her phone buzzed with a text.

Jett: I just got home but am on a call. Let yourself in.

"Of course he's working," she murmured quietly to herself. How different things were now that Jett had a wife and child. She used to spend countless hours alone at his home filling his fridge and cooking meals while Jett worked late at the office. He now had priorities just as important as his career. Lena and the nanny would come and go from the large property, but it wasn't like Jett's bachelor days in the least. He tried to work from home when he could, but she couldn't very well barge in unannounced and accidentally scare Anna. Their cameras had no doubt picked up her arrival, but Lena knew Anna didn't watch them closely in the way Jett did. He was the type of man who was always aware, just like Gray. Most men wouldn't want to cross them, but she knew plenty had tried. Inexplicably, she shivered.

Lena walked into the kitchen a few minutes later, her arms full of groceries. She set the bags on the counter, slid off her winter coat, and was unpacking when Jett stalked in. "Damn it all to hell," he muttered.

"Problems?" Lena asked lightly, moving around him to put a few things in the fridge.

He let out a sigh. "West is still trying to track down that bastard Ivan Rogers. It pisses me off that we don't have him yet."

"Gray looked stressed earlier," Anna commented, walking into the kitchen to stand beside her husband.

Lena rearranged a few things in the fridge and shot Anna a look. "He's worried about me."

"Well, I'm sure big, bad Gray can keep you safe. He's barely let you out of his sights," Anna teased. "Don't think I haven't noticed you two arriving at the office together every morning."

Jett's lips quirked as he ducked down to give Anna a quick kiss. "It's not like we took things slowly, sweetness."

"That we did not," Anna agreed, flashing him a knowing look. She glanced down and lightly rubbed her belly. "And you sure have trouble being good and keeping your hands to yourself."

Jett barked out a laugh, then glanced at his phone as another call came in. "Can you blame me?" he asked, his eyes sparking with heat as his gaze raked over his pregnant wife.

Lena knew her cheeks were turning pink as Jett strode out of the room. She really didn't need to hear anything about Jett and Anna's sex life. Given the racy lingerie and other gifts Jett sometimes requested she pick up, Lena had no doubt they were quite amorous. Plus, Anna was pregnant. Again. Clearly, they were a couple who couldn't keep their hands off of each other.

That didn't mean she needed Anna speculating about what Lena and Gray did every night.

Anna winked at Lena as Jett left the room. "What?" she asked innocently. "Gray was always watching you before. He's certainly quite attentive now, making sure you're safe every morning before work."

"And you thought you'd point this out to my boss?" Lena asked dryly, moving to unpack the rest of the groceries.

"Oh please. You're like family to Jett. And I love that you're finally getting some with the last single guy on the team," Anna teased, coming over to help unpack some of the groceries. "Gray sure looks like he knows how to please a woman in bed."

"You're incorrigible." Lena tried to bite back her smile, failing miserably. Gray did certainly know what he was doing in bed, and Lena had absolutely no complaints about that.

"That's why everyone loves me," Anna declared, her eyes twinkling.

Chapter 13

Gray strode in Lena's office after the team's briefing, worry coursing through him. They finally needed to move forward on the Mexico op, with Luke and Sam flying out first thing in the morning. It would be a quick reconnaissance mission for the moment, with the men returning before the weekend. The short trip wouldn't be a problem unless shit hit the fan. Then the entire team would be involved, except Gray knew he couldn't leave Lena alone. Not when Ivan Rogers was still out there somewhere.

She could stay at Anna's house. Stay at a hotel. But something in his gut told him he couldn't leave her. She'd even mentioned it felt like she was being watched the other night. West's team of IT guys had hacked into the security feed of the grocery store, but nothing unusual had been noted.

His steps slowed as he approached her desk,

something inside him settling now that he was near her. Lena's long, glossy hair hung down around her breasts. Her blazer was draped over the back of her chair, so he got an eyeful of her pretty cleavage.

His dick twitched.

Only this morning he'd buried his face in her breasts, kissing and laving at her pink nipples while he fingered her wet pussy. She'd moaned out his name, helpless to his advances and thorough touch. After he'd made Lena come twice, he'd made love to her, slow and sweet in bed. Seeing her dark gaze looking up at him, so trusting, had made something in his chest crack wide open.

This woman was it for him.

After they'd both come, he'd held her close in the quiet morning. Neither of them had wanted to move, both safe and happy in each other's arms, but they'd eventually showered together and dressed for work.

"Hey you," she said with a smile as she looked up from her computer screen, and Gray's thoughts shifted back to the present.

"Hey yourself," he said, ducking down for a quick kiss. They hadn't discussed how they'd act in the office around each other. Things had progressed naturally, and no one seemed surprised in the least when they were suddenly standing too close to one another or holding back for a brief moment to share a kiss. Jett was affectionate with Anna, so it wasn't exactly unprecedented. Gray knew he was probably the last guy anyone expected to be in a relationship.

They'd hadn't exactly discussed that either. One moment they were friends and colleagues, and the next? Lovers. Everything had changed since he'd rescued her weeks ago. While he hated that she'd endured any of that, he loved where they were now. He'd been on his own so long, dealing with his own troubles, he hadn't realized how much he'd been missing. Lena filled in the gaps and holes in his life in a way he didn't realize he'd needed. He'd recovered from his physical injuries, his body mostly healed, but he hadn't been complete.

"What are you up to?" Gray asked, watching as Lena scrolled through a webpage full of pink and blue baby decorations. "That's a far cry from ordering more Kevlar vests and ammo."

"I'm planning a baby shower for this weekend," she said, glancing up at him with a grin.

"This weekend? That's only a few days away," he said with a chuckle. "Why the rush?"

She shrugged. "Jett's request. Anna just found out they're having another boy, so she's really excited. Truth be told, I think he is, too, although he's way too macho and gruff to admit feeling sappy over a baby. Clara had her ultrasound this week, too, and found out that she and Ford are having a girl. They want to hold the party at their house, but it'll be a double baby shower that everyone's invited to. There's no baby registry, but people can of course bring something if they want. Clara claimed to already have what she needed and Jett and Anna obviously have a ton of baby stuff. It's more of a celebration I suppose than a true baby shower."

"Is it on Saturday?" Gray asked.

"Yeah, why?"

Gray cleared his throat. "I've got an appointment Saturday afternoon to bring my SUV in. Just an oil change and tire rotation, but it might take an hour or two."

"It's no biggie. You can stay over like usual, and then I'll be running around doing last-minute errands and prep in the afternoon. I'm ordering a ton of decorations and will overnight them to Ford and Clara's house. Clara's older daughter is excited and wants to help decorate for the party, so that gets me off the hook for that," she added with a laugh. "You can take care of your car while I'm picking up the food. Ford's going to grill, even though it's the middle of winter, but I'm getting a cake and ordering a huge platter of appetizers."

"I don't know," he said with a frown. "I could reschedule so I could help you."

"Don't be silly. I run errands for Jett all the time. I can easily handle the party. It's just for the team anyway. I'll grab the food myself if you're not back yet, and then we can head over together."

Gray frowned, and Lena stood up, wrapping her arms around his neck. Even in her heels, she was still slightly shorter than him, and he loved the feeling of her curves pressed up against his body. She rose to her tiptoes, and he met her for a heated kiss. "I want you to be safe," he murmured. "I'm already beating myself up for the coffee shop a month ago."

She pulled back slightly, staring into his eyes. "We've been over this. You can't be there every second. You're not my shadow," she joked.

"I could be," he growled, sucking in a breath. Just thinking about Lena scared and helpless was almost enough to send him into a tailspin. He could deal with his own shit, his own demons, but thinking about Lena being hurt killed him.

"And you'd just follow me into the ladies' room each time I needed to pee? I don't think so," she said, sliding her hands to his cheeks. "I love that you're protective of me, but those guys after Kaylee were pure evil. They would've found her one way or another, because just like you, Nick couldn't be at her side every single second. Unfortunately, I got caught in the crossfire, so to speak."

He squeezed her waist with his hands. "I fucking hate that they even touched you."

Lena bit her lip and nodded. "Me too, but in a weird, roundabout way it brought me to you."

A beat passed, Gray hating to admit what he knew to be true. If he hadn't helped Lena, he would've still been hanging out in the wings, only partly living his life. He would've missed out on this. Her. "You're right. And for that, I'm so damn thankful." Gray pulled her closer, one hand sliding up to the back of her head, his fingers threading through her hair. Then he kissed her thoroughly, not caring that they were at work, in her office, when anyone could walk in and see them. "You're it for me, Lena," he said when he pulled back, both of them breathing heavily. He could almost feel those three little words hanging in the air but didn't say them yet. It was too soon, but hell if he didn't feel that in his heart.

Gray was sure the expression on her face mirrored his own—full of wonder and something that had to be love.

"You're it for me, too," she said, before pulling him close for another kiss.

Minutes passed before they came up for air, their bodies pressed close and hearts beating as one. "We should continue this tonight," she teased, her gaze dropping to his erection straining against his pants.

"Yep," he managed to say through clenched teeth.

Lena giggled, patting him over his pants. "Down, boy."

"Not. Helping."

Voices in the hall drew her attention, and she winked. "I'll give you a moment. Jett's coming to talk with me more about the party. He's probably got some surprise for Anna in mind," she said with a laugh.

Muttering a curse, Gray watched her walk out the door, hips swinging in that tight skirt. Damn, he was a goner. He wouldn't have it any other way."

Chapter 14

"Oh no, that's frustrating it's taking so long," Lena said, holding her phone in one hand as she pushed a shopping cart through the store. "I already grabbed the cake and am picking up the platter I ordered. Did they give any indication if they're almost done with your car?"

Gray swore under his breath. "Yeah. Should be twenty minutes, tops."

"It'll be okay," Lena said. "Why don't I just meet you at Ford and Clara's house? I'll have all the food, and then you can head straight there from the auto shop. We'll both get there just about right on time."

"Yeah, I guess I'll have to do that," Gray said. "I wanted to go together, but if the food is ready, you don't want to be late because of me. We can't have the pregnant ladies starving," he joked.

"It'll be fine," Lena assured him. "The store's crowded, so by the time I drove home to meet you, we'd be running late anyway. I'll see you when I get there, okay baby?"

She could almost picture Gray relaxing at her words. "Yeah. Okay. Just be careful, all right? Some of the guys just got back from Mexico, and there's crazy shit going on everywhere in the world. I'd feel better if I was with you."

"I know, but it's the middle of the day, and I'm always out running errands. I promise I'll be careful. I'll see you soon, okay?"

"Okay, baby girl," he said, his voice husky.

"And tell those auto shop guys to hurry up," she joked. "I need to see my man tonight."

Gray chuckled, his voice lowering. "I know you do, baby." She felt tingles racing down her spine at his words. When they'd made love last night, Gray had enjoyed talking dirty as he'd teased her, dragging out the moment until she finally orgasmed. Gray had asked if she'd needed her man to fill her pretty pussy, and Lena had almost combusted on the spot. Lena wasn't used to that kind of dirty talk, but something about hearing the words in Gray's deep voice gave her a thrill. She didn't think she'd ever come so hard as when he'd finally sunk inside her, thrusting in hard and deep as she clung to him desperately.

The woman behind the counter brought her platter over, and Lena lifted the entire thing into her shopping cart. The large cake was below, ready to go, so she headed to the front of the store to check out. The line was slow, and she found herself watching the shoppers around her. Mothers. Kids. Men by themselves and couples pushing carts together.

The cashier scanned her items, and after Lena swiped her card, she was heading into the busy parking lot. Typically, she avoided the store on weekend afternoons. It was too crowded, crazy, and full of impatient drivers. There was already a long line at the main entrance, with traffic backed up at the stoplight.

She hurried through the parking lot, bracing against the dry, cold winter air. Upstate New York might be beautiful, but it was also bitterly cold this time of year. Sighing, she opened her trunk. It would've been more fun having Gray with her. Plus, he would've let her get inside the car to warm up while he loaded everything. He needed to get his errands done, too, so she could hardly fault him for being a responsible adult. Lena should probably think about making her own car appointment soon. She was overdue for an oil change herself.

Closing the trunk, she crossed the lot, her empty cart rattling loudly as she took it to the cart return. Her phone buzzed, and she saw a text from Jett.

Jett: Everything all set?

She quickly thumbed a response.

Lena: I just picked up the appetizers and cake. I'm on my way over right now.

Jett: Fantastic. And thanks for booking that maternity spa package for Anna. She was in heaven.

Shaking her head, she turned away from the cart return, walking back to her vehicle. Anna loved everything from Jett, and the fact that he loved bestowing presents on her was a thrill in and of itself. Lena didn't mind shopping for Anna, although it was more than a little amusing now that she knew the woman she was picking out things for. His weekend fling with Anna had been one thing, but now she was Lena's friend and Jett's wife.

Clicking her key fob to unlock her doors, Lena slowed as she saw something hanging from the side mirror on the driver's side. She didn't think anything had been there a moment ago, although she'd also been busy loading the food into the trunk.

"It's a breezy day, isn't it?" the man climbing into the truck next to her said with a leering look. He shut the door and started the engine, driving off before she could respond.

What in the—

Lena stilled, her gaze landing on something on the ground beside her door. Had the man dropped it? It almost looked like—

Zip ties.

They were linked around her side mirror as well, strung together like some creepy zip tie chain.

Fear churned through her as she took a step back. She should call someone. Jett. Gray. The police. Turning away, she could see the truck that had been parked beside her exiting the lot in the back. It had avoided the main entrance where all the traffic was.

What did that guy mean by saying it was a breezy day?

Alarm washed over her as she remembered the zip ties in her driveway. She'd been talking with her neighbors about the windy day and how they must've just blown over to her yard.

But—

"Hello Lena."

She froze, instantly trembling in place at the cold voice behind her. No. This couldn't be happening. No. No. No.

Quiet footsteps approached from behind, and Lena heard her own heart thundering in her ears. She was paralyzed in place, wanting to scream, to fight, to run, but unable to do a damn thing.

"Don't move, pretty girl," he said, a hint of laughter in his voice. He could no doubt see that she was literally shaking. "My men are already here. Waiting. Wanting a turn with what's mine." Her eyes darted around the lot, and she noticed several men were already closing in on her.

Ivan stopped right behind her, and she could smell his heavy cologne, feel the heat from his beefy body, and practically taste the stench of alcohol on his breath. "But I'm not sharing. It's time to finish what we started, beautiful," he said, his meaty hands pulling her close. Covering her mouth as she whimpered. "Except this time," he leered, grinding his erection against her ass as he held her in an iron-like grip, "you'll never get away from me. Never."

Chapter 15

Gray grabbed his keys from the clerk, muttering under his breath. He glanced at the clock on the wall, knowing he'd arrive late to the party. He didn't know what the hell the holdup had been. At one point, he'd thought about bumming a ride to Ford and Clara's, except then he'd be without his vehicle until Monday morning. The shop was closing soon and wasn't open on Sundays.

He swiped the screen on his phone as he walked to the parking lot, calling Lena. It rang and rang, but he knew she was busy picking up the cake and platter. As soon as her voicemail kicked in, he left a brief message. "Hey. I'm on my way to the party right now, baby girl. I'll see you soon. Call me back if you need help with the food. Bye."

He climbed into his SUV, smiling as he saw Lena's sweater in the backseat. He'd peeled it off her the other night and tossed it behind him, leaving her in her camisole as they made out in the parking lot. Silly as it sounded, the moment had been hot. Sometimes he felt like a damn teenager around her, his cock always at half-mast, his heart pounding madly. It wasn't just their chemistry though. Lena made him smile, made him feel more alive than he had in years. They'd gone for a short walk around her neighborhood the other evening, and holding her hand, tugging her close in the cool winter air? It had felt fucking right.

Damn. Gray was a goner. He could see a million more evenings like that—dinners and walks with Lena, laughter, heated nights in each other's arms. She even kept the ceiling fan on in her bedroom, temperature turned low, knowing Gray slept better with the feel of cool air washing over him. He had no trouble making sure she was warm enough, enjoying the feel of her curves pressed against him, their bodies skin to skin.

When he pulled onto Ford and Clara's street ten minutes later, he frowned. While multiple vehicles were in their driveway and along the road, Lena's wasn't among them. Neatly parallel parking, he climbed out of his vehicle and slammed the car door shut. Jett and Anna were across from him, apparently also running late as they got out of their own vehicle. "You hear from Lena?" he called out, a frown on his face.

Jett nodded, one arm wrapping around his pregnant wife. "She's on her way."

An inexplicable feeling of relief washed over him. Gray had no specific reason to be concerned right now, but worry still niggled at the back of his mind. She'd probably been loading the food into her car and couldn't talk right when he'd called. Gray pulled his phone free from his pocket, shooting her a text anyway.

Gray: Are you almost here? I just parked on the street and can help you carry stuff in.

There was no answer, and he paused for a beat, looking down the quiet road. The store was about ten minutes in the opposite direction from which he'd come. Lena had expected them to arrive at the same time, so she'd probably be here soon. Reluctantly, Gray followed Jett and Anna into the home.

Laughter erupted from his friends, and he glanced over to see Sam and Ava holding a ridiculously big stuffed animal. Nope. Make that two. Evidently, they'd gotten one for each expectant mother. He moved through his friends, saying hello, his eyes sweeping the space. A table had assorted sparkling waters set out for the pregnant women, plus soda, beers, and wine. A large section of the next table was empty, a post-it note in the middle with the word "App Platter" scrawled across, obviously saving room for what Lena was bringing. Cups and plates surrounded it, and he saw the plastics rings from a six-pack of soda cans, the trash reminding him of the zip ties in Lena's driveway.

Oddly enough, as many times as he'd driven to her home, he hadn't seen any construction debris blowing around from her neighbor's remodeling project.

He checked his texts, seeing no response, then tried Lena's number again. It still rang until it went to voicemail, and Gray frowned.

"All right, we're almost ready to start!" Clara called out, looking around the crowded living room. "Thank you so much to everyone for coming. Ford says he doesn't mind grilling in the dead of winter, and I've been too tired to do much cooking lately. Hopefully a winter barbeque is okay with everyone to celebrate."

"It's perfect," Sam said with a grin, standing to Gray's left with Ava. "I'm always ready to eat."

"You like to eat me," Ava whispered as she nudged him, causing Sam to choke back his laughter.

"Damn straight, woman."

"I'll put the burgers on in a few minutes. We can't have the pregnant ladies going hungry," Ford joked. He looked toward the table of food near Gray. "Where's the appetizer platter?" Ford asked. "I thought Lena was picking it up."

"I actually don't think she's here yet," Clara said, looking around at their group of friends.

"She's not," Gray said, a sudden feeling of alarm coursing through him. Lena wouldn't be late for this. She was meticulous in her planning. If she'd had car trouble or some other issue, she'd have texted him.

"She left more than thirty minutes ago," Jett said. "Lena texted me to say she was on her way over."

Gray's phone began to buzz with a text, and much to his alarm, he realized his teammates phones were buzzing as well. He swallowed back the sudden lump in his throat, the hair on the back of his neck standing up. His hands were almost shaking as he swiped the screen. Something was wrong. He knew it.

He stared at the message in disbelief.

Unknown: I took back what's mine.

"What the hell?" Nick asked.

There were other low murmurs amongst his friends, a sudden feeling of concern in the air.

"Has anyone talked to Lena?" Jett barked.

"I can't reach her," Anna said from his side,

looking slightly frazzled. "I just tried her cell and the office. There was no answer. Call her home number."

Jett was already dialing it, muttering as the phone went to her voicemail.

Gray's phone buzzed again and again, and his stomach dropped as he scanned over the texts.

There was a photo of Lena in her lingerie, tied to a bed, a gag over her mouth. He didn't miss the absolute fear in her eyes. The tears streaming down her cheeks.

The text that came next nearly made his heart stop.

Unknown: I want $50 million for the trouble you've caused. Pay up or I'll slit her throat.

Unknown: I almost took her the night you showed up.

Unknown: Lena is mine now.

"They took her!" Gray choked out, anguish filling every fiber of his being. "I just got a photo of Lena and a ransom note. That monster took Lena!"

The entire team was moving then, rushing to his side. Jett took the phone, scanning over the texts. He was already calling West on his own phone to track the origin of the messages. Gray felt his legs shaking, his entire body shutting down. He'd fucking failed her. He'd failed the woman he loved.

She was back in the hands of a monster.

Chapter 16

"You're even prettier than I remembered," Ivan leered, reaching out to touch Lena's hair. His big hand slid down her cheek, her neck, until he was lewdly groping at her breasts. Tears streamed down her face, and she heard chuckles from the men who'd been driving the big black SUV. They were just as eager as Ivan to hurt her.

Bile rose in the back of her throat as Ivan pulled her closer to him, his meaty hands pawing at her everywhere.

Ivan hadn't forced her into the backseat with him, but it was only when he'd threatened to hunt down and kill her pregnant friend that she'd gone without a fight.

Lena had shuddered at the realization that Ivan knew who Anna was. Had he been watching them in the coffee shop a month ago? But no. That couldn't be right. It was only after Kaylee had mistakenly used

143

her credit card on her phone's app that they'd found her, and Anna was long gone by then. Yet somehow, Ivan had followed Lena. Found her. And he knew who her friends were as well.

Trembling, she wondered if he'd seen her with Gray.

Her gaze darted around the heavily wooded area as they stood outside the SUV. They'd driven a short distance from the shopping center to a secluded home in the woods, and Ivan had gloated about the days he'd spent watching her. Waiting. Jacking off in his vehicle as he imagined fucking her.

Lena wanted to vomit.

She looked around the forest, shivering in the winter air, and desolation washed over her. Gray wouldn't be able to quickly find her. He didn't even know she was missing yet. They'd have to figure out what grocery store she'd gone to, locate her car.... She sniffled, unable to stop the tears falling down her face. Even then, it might take hours. Days. Ivan could have taken her anywhere by then—out of New York. Out of the country. Away from the man she loved.

More tears spilled down her cheeks. She hadn't even told Gray how she felt about him. When he eventually found her car in the parking lot, he'd see her keys and winter coat on the ground, the latter ripped off her by Ivan. He'd laughed as he'd threatened to strip her right there, raping her in front of his men.

Lena knew she should have screamed. Fought. Yelled as loudly as she could for help. But as soon as they'd mentioned Anna, she'd froze. Lena had no idea how many men Ivan had working for him, but she knew the evil he was capable of. His men had closed in on her, and she'd let them. Now, as a chill seeped into her bones, she knew she'd never get away.

"Go through her purse!" Ivan ordered, marching her into the secluded home, his grip on her arm unyielding.

His fingers dug further into her arm, and suddenly she panicked. He was going to hurt her. Rape her. Probably kill her. She'd never see Gray or any of her friends again. Lena let out a bloodcurdling scream, even knowing no one was around to hear. She screamed again, and Ivan roared in anger, lifting her up into his arms, the other men rushing to his aid. She fought and cried, but they were too strong, easily overpowering her.

One of the men was already pulling out her wallet, phone, and lipstick, tossing them onto the table as she fought in vain against Ivan. Someone slammed the front door shut, turning the lock, and Lena cried as Ivan forced her down the hallway. She cowered back as Ivan unceremoniously dumped her on the bed, his hands already moving to undo his belt buckle.

He wasn't going to wait around this time. He was going to rape her right here in front of the others. Two men appeared in the bedroom doorway, and Lena began to shake in fear. Would they all take turns assaulting her? She'd never let them. She'd rather die than be hurt that way.

"Get the contacts on her phone," Ivan ordered, whipping his belt off and flinging it to the ground.

One of the men swiped at the screen, frowning. "It's got a passcode."

Ivan turned to Lena, sneering as he stalked closer. "Tell him the numbers. I'm demanding payment from those assholes you work with. They want you back?

145

They've fucking ruined me! The Feds seized my assets because of them. Raided my homes. Stole from me. They'll fucking pay for this!"

Blinking at him in shock, she froze.

"Unlock it right now, or my men get a turn with you first!" he threatened.

Disgust and fear dueled within her. The other men looked like buzzards circling over a recent kill. Predators. And she was their prey.

The man holding the phone leered at her, his gaze lingering on her breasts. Lena had worn a pretty dress for the baby shower, a new one that Gray would love. He'd never see her in it, she realized, the thought ridiculous at the moment.

Ivan licked his lips, his eyes raking up and down Lena, and she could see the outline of his erection pressing against his pants. He was excited from watching them manhandle her. From throwing her onto the bed, knowing she couldn't escape. His gaze ran over her body lasciviously, and in that split second, Lena knew he was never letting her go. He'd kill her before he allowed anyone to save her. Maybe he'd taken a sick liking to her a month ago, but now? He was out for blood. Revenge. Whatever Gray and his teammates had started with the Feds had escalated far beyond Ivan's control. He'd take it out on her, then kill her if she was lucky.

Lena swallowed, the entire room feeling like it was beginning to spin. At least if Ivan contacted Shadow Security, Gray would know for certain who had her. It would at least give him a chance to find her. She recited the numbers to unlock her phone as Ivan threatened her again, and then he was chuckling. Hovering over her like the devil himself.

"Take off your dress!" he ordered.

"What? No!" she cried out, horror washing through her.

"You're mine now," Ivan told her, a crazed look filling his eyes. "I had a girl like you once before. Pretty. Brunette. Perfect pouty lips. When I saw you all those weeks ago, I knew you'd be the perfect replacement. Big tits. Wide eyes. A mouth that's begging to be fucked. A curvy, luscious body that belongs to me now."

Lena screamed as Ivan lunged at her, and then he was ripping her dress off, pinning her wrists to the mattress and ordering his men to tie her down so she couldn't escape. Lena kicked and screamed, and then he tied her ankles to the bedframe as well, his leering gaze on her body. Tears ran down her cheeks as he pulled out a knife, holding it up menacingly.

"Don't make me use this!"

Shaking, she quieted, unable to fight Ivan as he gagged her. Grabbing Lena's unlocked phone from his men, Ivan snapped a picture of her crying on the bed in nothing but her bra and panties. He laughed as he scrolled through her contacts. "I'll send this photo to the men you work with along with my demands. I think they'll enjoy the picture," he sneered, his eyes filling with lust as they raked over her. "It'll be the last time any of them ever sees you again."

***

Gray ran his hands through his short hair, frantic. This couldn't be happening. It couldn't. He'd just seen Lena earlier. Kissed her goodbye before he took his car in for an oil change. Spoken with her on the phone with plans to meet at Ford and Clara's. She was just picking up the food. She was supposed to be okay.

And now she was gone, kidnapped by the same twisted predator who'd taken her before.

Devastation roiled through him, making it hard to breathe. Gray sucked in some air, panic nearly overtaking him. He needed to keep his shit together, but his own nightmares were coming back, the memories crippling. He'd been held captive, too. He'd been tortured. Helpless.

And now that same damn thing was happening to Lena.

"No!" he roared, his hands clenched in menacing fists. The room stopped, looking at him.

"We're going to find her," Jett said, clapping him on the shoulder. Gray let out a breath and looked at his boss, seeing the pure rage behind Jett's calm demeanor. Jett was always in control, the epitome of cool, calm, and collected. This time, however, it was personal. Jett had known Lena longer than any of them, and Gray didn't miss the absolute anger boiling within his boss.

Gray nodded, too angry to speak.

"Where was Lena picking up the food?" Jett asked, his eyes alert.

Gray swallowed, realizing he didn't even know. "I'm not sure."

"Oh, I think at the market on Jefferson St.!" Anna called out, rushing over. "I mentioned that I love the cakes there."

Jett nodded, eyeing the team that had gathered around him. "We know she made it there because of the text she sent earlier. She had the food. We need a couple guys to head over there, but we also need to get with West. While the text the team received was anonymous, everything about this points to Ivan Rogers."

"On it, boss," Luke said, signaling to Ford.

"We'll head to the shopping center," Ford said. "There's got to be security cameras there. Witnesses."

"Her car," Gray choked out. "If she picked up the food but never left, her car might be there."

Jett was already nodding. "I know she got the platter and cake. The store will have surveillance cameras. Was she being followed? Watched? Did she leave the premises? We don't know if she was taken in the parking lot or already on her way here and ambushed."

"I'm going with them," Gray said, anger pulsing through his bloodstream. "If that was the last known location of Lena, I want to be there. I want to find her car."

"We could also check her home," Nick said, eyeing Gray. "Presumably, she was headed right to Ford and Clara's place, but what if she changed her plans?"

"Shit. You're right," Gray muttered. The zip ties. The fucking zip ties he'd found in her driveway. Was someone watching her then? Gray wanted to be everywhere at once, but that couldn't exactly happen. He'd have to rely on his teammates, just like on any other op. Except this was the most difficult mission of his life. They'd rescued Lena from hell once before, but now he'd kissed her, slept with her body pressed against his own, made love to her. Dizziness nearly overtook him.

"Take a deep breath," Sam said, coming to stand

by his side. "You're the strongest man on the team for the hell you went through, but Lena needs you right now."

He ground his teeth, nodding. His buddy was right. Gray needed to pull himself together. Imagining the worst wouldn't help his girl. He needed a clear head. A laser sharp focus. Every minute counted.

"I'm okay," he said, eyeing Jett and his teammates. "Don't bench me on this."

"Not a chance. Time is on our side," Jett said, echoing his thoughts. "Lena's been gone thirty minutes, tops. We need to find out where they took her. Where they're headed. If they move her to another location, it complicates the hell out of things."

"Let's roll," Ford said.

Gray was already turning, rushing to the front door.

"I'm driving!" Luke yelled.

Gray didn't argue. Ford was climbing into his own vehicle, which made sense, but Gray would ride with Luke. If they discovered any clues or hints as to where Lena had been taken, they might need to split up. Gray wasn't exactly in his right mind to obey traffic laws and road safety. Rage coursed through him, but with each second that passed, an eerie feeling of calm began to set in. He could compartmentalize his thoughts, focusing only on the mission. Gray was in the zone, and nothing mattered other than retrieving their package from the tangos. The fact that it was Lena? He'd have to sort through those emotions later. She needed him, and he couldn't fall apart now.

Ten minutes later, Luke's tires squealed as he tore

into the parking lot. Gray's gaze swept the area. Cars lined the spaces; shoppers pushed their carts full of groceries. Ford pulled in behind them, rolling to a stop at the curb in front of the store.

"Do you see her vehicle?" Luke asked, beginning to circle the lot.

"Not yet. I'm looking." Gray's phone buzzed in his hand. "Yeah?"

"I'm going to go speak with the manager and ask about the camera footage," Ford said. "If they won't help us, guess that's another thing West will hack into."

"Roger that."

Gray was already sliding back into the mode of an operator. They might not be on foreign soil, tracking down terrorists, but they'd approach the kidnapping with the same focus and intensity. Just because they weren't in uniform anymore didn't mean they weren't still an elite team of former soldiers.

"Does Jett have her license plate number?" Luke asked.

"Negative. If Lena's car is here, we'll relay that intel to the team. West can track her movements this afternoon on the traffic cams and see if she was being followed. Of course, if we have footage of her being abducted in the parking lot—"

He cut off. He didn't want to watch that, but if she'd been forced into a vehicle, they needed a description of it. A plate number.

"We'll find her," Luke assured him.

Gray clenched his jaw. He didn't doubt they'd find her eventually, but in what condition? Ivan Rogers had toyed with Lena before, drugging and groping her. Taunting her with all the disgusting ways he wanted to use her body. Gray had the horrible feeling that if Ivan got his hands on her again, he wouldn't mess around this time. Would Lena be raped? Killed?

Nausea roiled through him.

"There!" he shouted, suddenly spotting her car in an end row. It wasn't necessarily secluded, but it wasn't in the middle of the parking lot either. If they'd abducted her right from the lot, it would be the perfect location.

Luke sped up, his car racing down the row to her vehicle.

Gray jumped out, leaving the passenger door open as he rushed toward Lena's car. His stomach dropped as he saw her coat lying on the ground, and shit. Were those goddamn zip ties hanging from her side mirror? It's like they'd put them there to taunt her.

His mind flashed back to the night he'd arrived at her home. The zip ties in the driveway. Lena thinking she'd heard something go bump in the night. Had that bastard Ivan Rogers been watching her all this time?

Gray bent and picked up her coat, her floral scent slamming into him. A torrent of memories accosted him. Lena was good and sweet and pure. Innocent.

She was now in the hands of monsters.

"We should check inside the vehicle," Luke said, his voice grim. He palmed the keys that had been discarded on the ground beside the coat, frowning at the zip ties lying on the ground. Gray nodded, feeling sick, but watched as his buddy popped the trunk. Relief, sharp and instant, washed over him as he saw only the food Lena had picked up. The cake. The party platter. Aside from her personal things found on the ground, there wasn't a sign of a struggle. There was no blood on the pavement. No broken glass. No markings at all on the vehicle, just those fucking zip ties. And Lena wasn't inside the trunk of her car, forced in there by Ivan or his men. Gray had been half terrified that they'd find her body.

Lena had simply vanished.

Luke was already scanning the parking lot. "I'm going to speak with Ford and the grocery store manager. Let's review the surveillance footage, focusing on this area of the lot. If we know who took her, West can check the traffic cams. If they were on foot, we'll have a description of the men. They had to usher her somewhere, and there's a number of businesses around who no doubt have their own surveillance systems."

"We have no idea where she is," Gray choked out. The cool winter air bit into him, and for once, he hated the chill, the cold air on his skin. Lena was out there without her own coat, being held against her will. Was she cold? Scared? Hungry or injured?

Luke gripped his shoulder, giving it a firm squeeze. "We're going to find her. Lena is tough as hell. She'll stay strong until we get to her."

"She shouldn't have to go through any of this," Gray said with a shake of his head. "Go find Ford. I'll search the area around her car for any additional clues. Let's check with any witnesses on a possible description of the vehicle. The SUVs they drove in the first abduction were seized by the Feds or destroyed in the propane tank explosion."

"Pretty sure those belonged to Cronin and Levins anyway," Luke said. "Rogers no doubt has his own vehicles. He got away the first time."

"He sure as fuck won't get away now," Gray

seethed. His phone buzzed, and he saw Jett's name flash on the screen. "Yeah, boss?"

"West got a ping on the location of Lena's cell phone."

"What?" he asked in shock.

"The anonymous texter had all of our cell numbers. He sent her photo to the entire team. Lena is bright, but she's not going to have the number of every single man on the team memorized. Even if she did, she's under extreme duress."

"He has her cell phone."

"Affirmative. I asked West to track the origin of the anonymous texts, but we quickly realized that Ivan Rogers must have her cell phone with him—or he did at some point."

Gray scanned the area by her car again, surprised at what he'd missed. Lena always carried her purse with her. He opened her door, looking at the driver's side and passenger seat, then the back. They'd already looked inside the trunk. "Her purse isn't here either. He must have taken it when he abducted her."

"In the off-chance he uses her credit cards, we can use those to track them as well. Meanwhile, we got a ping off a cell tower approximately twenty minutes away."

"What's the location?" Gray asked.

Jett rattled off the coordinates of the tower, located in a small shopping center on a highway leading out of town. "We don't know where she is," he stressed. "Just the location of the tower. They could've moved on to another spot since then or turned off her phone. West and his team will keep tracking it to see if it pings again."

"Thanks boss. We'll head that direction while Ford

gets the surveillance footage here. We need every possible lead to get Lena back."

"West's team can hack into those traffic cams as well," Jett said, his voice hard. "We'll rescue Lena from those monsters and nail Ivan Rogers' ass to the wall, ending his entire operation."

Chapter 17

Ivan laughed manically, holding another cell phone in his hand. "I told your boyfriend and boss that I want $50 million for you." He chuckled darkly, handing the phone to one of his men. "Take a photo of me holding the knife to her throat," he ordered. "I promised that I'd kill her myself if they didn't come up with the money."

Lena sobbed as Rogers came toward her again, the sharp metal of the knife biting into her skin as he held it to her neck. "Smile pretty for the camera. Oh wait—you can't. You look good bound and gagged." Rogers trailed one hand down her body as she shook in fear.

"Got it," the guy with the phone said, smirking as he looked at her. "She's a pretty one. I bet she could take both of us at once."

Ivan's gaze swiveled toward the man, rage crossing his face. "Send the photo! And get the hell out so I can enjoy my prize."

The man muttered and stalked out of the bedroom as Ivan turned to stare at her once more, his gaze glossing over. "I'm not going to drug you this time, my pretty little jewel," he said. "I'm going to spend hours enjoying you, letting you suck me off real good before I fuck you. I know you want it. Look at you already trembling in anticipation."

Lena froze, and his dark laughter filled the bedroom. A new wave of fear washed over her. Ivan just wanted to scare her. He wouldn't really assault her for hours. If he was going to rape her, hopefully he'd get off and get the hell out.

"Cat got your tongue?" Ivan asked, seemingly delighted with his supposed cleverness. "You look good with a gag in your mouth, but you'll look even better sucking on my cock." Ivan crossed the room to slam the door, then returned to her, wrapping one meaty hand around her throat. He squeezed gently, and Lena began trembling in fear. "Be good for me," he admonished, "or I'll have to choke you until you pass out. Turn you over to my men when I'm done. They'd rip you to pieces," he added with a hard laugh.

He bent over her, and she could smell the stench of his heavy cologne and alcohol on his breath. "Good girl," Ivan said, his lips at her ear. "You dressed so pretty for me today," he said, leering at her breasts in the black lacy bra she wore. Then he was kissing and biting at her neck, slobbering all over her. "Maybe I'll bite your pretty breasts next, leave my mark all over you. Then I'll fuck you until you know exactly who you belong to now."

Lena quaked with terror as his teeth nipped at her skin again, then jolted in surprise as the bedroom door suddenly swung open, slamming into the wall.

"They're coming!" one of the men yelled as he rushed into the room, phone in his hand, eyes wide with alarm.

Ivan jerked away from her, rage crossing his face. "What? We just got here!"

"They're on the main road. Two vehicles just pulled into the parking lot at the strip mall. Big guys, probably former military. I think they're looking at a map. Brown was on lookout and just called me. We wanted to make sure we weren't followed here, but they're closing in."

"Fucking hell!" Ivan raged. "I didn't even get to enjoy her yet!"

Hope suddenly bloomed within Lena's chest. Her cell phone. Ivan had made her unlock it to get the team's contact info, but it had been turned on when they'd driven out here, neatly tucked in her purse. Gray and his teammates were tracking her. Coming for her. She knew it was them.

"We have to accelerate the plan," Ivan said, his crazed lust disappearing as a calculated look crossed his face. "Pity, because we were just getting started. Let's move her. Call the others to tell them we're on our way."

Lena whimpered as one of the men grabbed the knife, but then he was cutting her free from the ropes. Ivan stood at the dresser, his back to her, but then was crossing the room toward her with a syringe. "Hold her in place." His eyes landed on hers, glittering with excitement. "Sorry my little jewel. Looks like I'll have to drug you again after all. We'll have so much fun together when you wake up."

Rough hands held her down, and then she felt the

prick of a needle, her world beginning to fade as Ivan loomed over her. "Don't forget this one is mine," he scolded his men as their hands began to wander.

No. No. No.

This wasn't happening again.

Lena succumbed to the darkness.

Chapter 18

"We need to split up," Nick said, holding a satellite imagery printout of the area. "Aside from this shopping center and the older cluster of homes across the street, it's heavily wooded, getting more rural as the main road leads out of town."

Gray's stomach dropped. The road also led to a main artery, which meant Ivan Rogers could be anywhere with Lena. Heading toward Canada. Heading south into New York City. Traveling east toward Connecticut. Would they keep Lena here for their own sick purposes or move her? West had finally gotten the records of Ivan's private flights, but the team was still in the first stages of analyzing that data. The Shadow Ops Team couldn't fly to multiple cities, hoping that's where Ivan Rogers was. They needed solid intel. A course of action. A goddamn plan. Just because Ivan sold women from various cities in his sex-trafficking ring didn't mean he'd take

Lena there either. Not when he was on the run and wanted her that badly.

"How the hell did you get sat imagery so fast?" Luke asked in surprise, looking at the map Nick was holding.

"West had one of his guys bring it over to Ford's house. He pulled it up as soon as he got a ping on Lena's cell. His team is looking over satellite images from the past few days to determine if there's been an uptick of movement in the area. Vehicles. Trucks hauling merchandise."

Gray's stomach dropped. The only merchandise Ivan moved was women.

"Given it's slightly rural, there's a chance we could get lucky and find a cluster of vehicles on a side road that aren't usually traveling that route," Nick explained. "That doesn't help us see the homes in those forested sections, however. We need boots on the ground for that. Let's divide up and search ourselves, driving down all these sideroads. Ivan doesn't work alone. He has a vast network, and if he's here, there's likely a team of guys with him."

"There were numerous vehicles at the home Lena was held at before," Gray said, his voice low.

"Exactly. Spotting something like that again could be a big tip off as to where he's holed up."

Luke looked up from the printout, eyeing Nick. "And her cell hasn't pinged again since earlier?"

"Negative," Nick said with a frown.

"Given the highway this road leads to and the multiple cell towers they'd pass on the way, they damn well might still be in the area," Gray said. "Or else they turned off her phone, and we're fucked," he added darkly. That was a thought he hardly wanted to consider, because then they'd rushed over here for nothing and Lena was being taken farther and farther away from him with each second that passed.

His eyes caught on a pickup truck at the far edge of the lot, the man in the driver's seat looking right at them. Gray opened his mouth to tell his teammates when his phone buzzed. He muttered a curse as he got a new text, noticing that truck started its engine and slowly drove away.

"Can you read those plates?" he asked, nodding toward the truck. It wasn't speeding out of there but still felt suspicious. The lot was mostly empty. Why was he watching them?

"Hang on," Luke said, rummaging through his bag and pulling out a pair of binoculars. The men all kept go-bags in their trunks with changes of clothes and basic gear. At the moment, Gray was thankful as hell they did. Luke rattled off the plate number as Nick scrawled it down, the truck pulling onto the road.

Gray's phone continued buzzing, and he scanned over the texts.

Anonymous: You have 24 hours. $50 million or you never see the girl again.

Anonymous: I'll provide you the number of an offshore account to wire the money. Clock's ticking.

Anonymous: Maybe I'll send her offshore when I'm finished with her.

Anonymous: Best pussy I've ever had.

"Fuck!" Gray shouted. He turned, punching into nothing but thin air. He wanted to beat the shit out of someone. Wring that guy's neck and then burn his entire enterprise to the ground. Destroy every molecule in his body. If Ivan dared hurt Lena, Gray didn't care if he himself ended up behind bars. He'd murder Ivan Rogers along with all of the men terrorizing her.

"What's wrong?" Nick asked, looking up from the plate number he'd just written down.

Gray held up his phone, letting his teammates read the texts, when the other men's phones began buzzing as well. Luke swore as a photograph of Lena appeared, and Gray nearly choked as he looked at the image. Lena was still bound to the bed, terrified, but this time a man's hand was holding a knife to her throat.

"He's going to kill her. Ivan threatened to slit her throat, and it looks like he goddamn might," Gray said, his voice rising. "He'll dump her body offshore afterwards."

"He's goading you," Luke said. "Trying to get a rise out of you to throw us off. She's restrained and helpless. He's more concerned with photographing her to taunt us than doing anything else at the moment. He wants his money."

"You don't know that."

"He could've easily hurt her by now. Assaulted her. Killed her. Why all the texts? The photos? It's just a sick, twisted game to him."

Gray briefly calmed, remembering Lena's words from the initial kidnapping. Ivan had enjoyed playing with her. Drugging her. Was that what this was about? Another twisted power play by Ivan? He thrived on other people's fear. He'd built an entire career of selling flesh. Innocent women. His taunts could just be meaningless drivel at this point, meant to upset the team into thinking he'd already assaulted Lena. But what was his end game?

Gray had no doubt he'd eventually rape and kill

her. He could only hope neither had happened yet.

"How old is this photo?" Gray asked urgently.

Nick shook his head. "Don't know. It's probably in the photo properties. Does that come through on a text? I don't know if the data is accurate."

"Call West," Luke said.

The other men continued talking, Gray's mind racing. It had been nearly an hour since anyone had heard from Lena. An entire fucking hour. In the thirty minutes after she'd texted Jett that she was on her way, she'd been abducted. And it felt like they were barely any closer to finding her. Sure, they'd discovered her vehicle, but the priority was Lena herself. She was missing, and he wanted to claw his own heart out thinking about whatever pain she was enduring. When he found her, and Gray swore that he would, he'd do everything in his power to show her just how much she meant to him.

"What if they drove right past this area?" Gray asked as he looked down the road, fresh concern coursing through him. "We could be standing around while they're getting away."

"West didn't get any other pings on her cell," Nick reminded him. "Maybe they wised up and turned it off, maybe not. Do you really want to take your chances with leaving when we could be searching the surrounding roads and forest? There are multiple one-lane roads around here, leading to secluded homes. That's similar to where we found Lena and Kaylee before—a house off the beaten path, used for Ivan's sick purposes."

"Let's search the surrounding area," Luke said in a clipped tone. "We need to find him ASAP before this comes to a head. Has anyone texted him back? Or is the number spoofed so that we can't even reply to his bullshit?"

"Jett texted him," Gray said, his voice low and deadly. "He's leading 'anonymous' to believe we're cooperating and coming up with the funds to spare Lena's life."

"Perfect," Luke quipped. "Because if Ivan thinks we're playing his game, he'll never see us coming." Luke's phone buzzed just then, and he lifted it to his ear, his gaze sharp. "Got it, boss. Putting you on speaker."

Jett's voice came over the line as the other men gathered close. "We've got a description of the vehicles from the parking lot," Jett said. "Ford obtained the surveillance footage from outside the grocery store. West will get into the local traffic cams to see if they passed your current location. If not, they're likely still in the area."

"You got the plates, boss?" Luke asked.

"Affirmative." Jett rattled them off, and Gray felt his blood run cold, looking at the plate number Nick had just written down.

"The truck—" Gray cut off as all of the men began running, jumping into their vehicles. Luke was still talking to Jett, informing him about the pickup truck they'd just spotted, but Gray barely heard a word.

"It went south!" Nick shouted before climbing into his own vehicle, slamming the door shut behind him.

Luke's tires squealed as he peeled out of the lot. Jett ended the call, saying he'd get an update from West. "We've got to be close," Gray said, drumming his fingers on the door. "Hell. He was driving slowly so we wouldn't be suspicious. He couldn't have gotten far at the rate he was going."

Ford pulled up to a guy stopped on a motorcycle, asking if he'd seen a pickup truck come through. The man pointed toward an intersection farther down the road. And there it was. A lone vehicle off in the distance heading toward the forest.

"That can't be him," Gray said with a frown.

"Only one way to find out," Luke said, revving the engine. He gunned it down the road, Nick speeding up behind him.

Luke's tires squealed as he took a turn, and then he was racing forward again. Gray frowned as they got closer, his stomach dropping. It wasn't the same truck. "We need to get into the traffic cams to see which way it headed."

Luke's phone began ringing, and he pushed the button on his console to answer the call via his car's system. "It's West," a male voice said without preamble. "I just got another ping from Lena's cell."

"Tell me it's nearby," Gray said.

"Negative. They're headed east, possibly looking to get on 95 south."

"What?" Gray yelled as Luke slammed on the brakes. He executed a neat three-point turn on the rural road, revving his engine as he sped back in the direction they'd just come. Nick was turning around as well, racing behind them to catch up.

"Let's hope they keep her phone on," West said. "It's a stupid mistake, but one that benefits us. As long as they're in range of a cell tower, I'll know the direction they're headed. I'm running the plates through our systems as well, trying to find them on a traffic cam. We'll know if they enter or exit the highway."

"He's getting away with her," Gray said, anguished.

"Not exactly," West countered. "As long as he has both Lena and her phone, he's leading us right to them."

Chapter 19

Tears streamed down Lena's cheeks as Ivan manhandled her yet again, yanking her out of the vehicle. She was shaking in the darkness, wearing her ripped dress over her bra and panties. She cringed knowing Ivan had touched her while she was passed out. He'd dressed her. Carried her, unconscious, to the car.

Gray had carried her in his arms to safety, but Ivan?

It was like he was leading Lena to her grave.

She wasn't sure how long she'd been out, but she suspected that hours had passed. Lena had briefly come to as they transferred her to a new vehicle, the light waning. The sky was dark now, the stars bright. Her stomach roiled with nausea, and her mouth was dry and felt like it was filled with cotton.

Blinking, she realized the gag was gone. Did that mean no one was around to hear her scream? Lena swayed on her feet, Ivan chuckling as he pulled her close. His cologne made her want to vomit, and just looking at him repulsed her.

"Don't fight me," he warned. Ivan reached out and gripped her chin, forcing her to look up at him. Lena was too weak and slow in her thinking from being drugged to try to push him away. "You really are my perfect little jewel. Prettier than the other girls. You'll fetch a mighty sum for me."

She stumbled, nearly falling over as he laughed. "While I planned to keep you, you've become far too much trouble for me now. I'll collect my $50 million and find some other girls to fuck."

"You're crazy," she mumbled.

Lena gasped as he slapped her across the face. While he was unhinged, he hadn't actually hurt her yet. Groped her, drugged her, yes. But hit her? Lena's cheek stung as fresh tears fell. It was dark and cold, and even if she tried to run, where could she go?

Ivan gripped her arm more tightly, no doubt leaving a bruising mark.

She shook from fear and the cold as he moved her along through some industrial buildings, the other men following behind them. She had no idea where they were, but it seemed that it was no longer New York. By now Gray would certainly be looking for her. He'd have found her car. The zip ties. At least Gray would realize someone had been watching her. Stalking her. It wasn't a coincidence that the zip ties had been outside her home.

Ivan's gaze swept to his men. "Do you still have her phone? Trash it. I'm already in communication with the head of the company she works for. They might be in the security business, but they're not bright enough to outsmart me."

The man muttered something, and Ivan swore. "They nearly found us earlier, but it actually worked in my favor," Ivan said with a dark laugh. "By the time they show up here, you'll be long gone. We'll ambush them, I'll get my millions wired offshore, and you'll already be on your way." His eyes glimmered with evil as he looked down at her. "I've got a special buyer for you. He likes it a little rough, but you should be able to take it. I'll even ship you there in your own private...accommodations."

Lena frowned, trying to work out what he was implying. Something was very off about this entire situation, but her mind was too slow from being drugged earlier to fully process it. They didn't seem to be near an airport because there weren't planes taking off or landing. They'd stopped driving. Was he just going to march her somewhere, handing her off to another man who was nothing but pure evil?

Her heart stopped as they turned a corner, moving around the last of the warehouses. There, floating in the distance, was a massive container ship stacked with cargo, the lights of the city harbor glimmering behind it.

"No."

She stumbled as she tried to stop, but Ivan pulled her along, chuckling.

"I wanted you for myself, but plans change. Most girls I take don't have anyone come looking for them, let alone a team of mercenaries. You're exactly what my buyer wants. Pretty. Curvy. Fuckable. I find all the prettiest girls," he chortled, letting his hands roam over her and giving her breasts a squeeze. "He'll use you until there's nothing left. I'll find a pretty brunette with big tits who looks just like you to keep for myself."

His laughter filled the air, and then Ivan's men were gripping her arms, hauling her away from him.

"I bet she's a screamer," one of the men said, giving her a slap on the ass.

A worker drove up on a maintenance vehicle, eyeing them with glee. He climbed out and spoke with Ivan, pocketing the money that Ivan slid into his palm. "We'll make sure she gets there in one piece," the man said with a smirk.

"Put her in the container ASAP. The ship is sailing at dawn, and I want my buyer to get exactly what he wants," Ivan ordered. "She can't be out here in the open if Shadow Security shows up."

"Got it, boss. I'll load her up like the others." His eyes landed on Lena, smirking, and he pulled out several zip ties as the other men forced her wrists together. She tried to fight them, her movements clumsy and uncoordinated. They tightened the plastic around her wrists, the edges cutting into her skin. Lena shrieked, finally letting out a bloodcurdling scream as she found her voice.

Rough arms snared around her, one of the men covering her mouth with his dirty hand. She fought against him, crying, but it was useless.

"You can scream all you want, honey," the guy driving the maintenance truck said. "No one will hear you in there."

***

"That can't be right," Gray said, staring at the coordinates West had given the team. They'd all convened at headquarters, gathering equipment and gear to roll out the second West gave them a definitive direction the vehicles were traveling. It felt like they were wasting precious time as it was, but they needed weapons. Kevlar vests. Night vision goggles. Tactical gear. If they were charging in somewhere to save her, they wouldn't be doing a half-assed job.

Lena's phone must have been turned off, because while there'd been nothing for hours, West had just now tracked the pings of Lena's cell all the way down to Baltimore. It was an odd choice given that Ivan typically traveled to Mexico or cities along the southern border. Even if he was traveling by car, Baltimore wasn't exactly a stop along the way. "What the hell's he doing in the Inner Harbor?" Gray wondered.

"Maybe he stopped for some Maryland crabs," Sam said.

"It's the goddamn middle of the night!" Gray yelled.

"Easy," Sam said, holding up his hands. "There are seafood markets that sell their fresh catch in the early morning. While the fishermen might make an honest living, I doubt they're the only dealers working at that hour."

"You think he's prostituting her?" Ford asked, anger lacing his own voice.

"I don't know what to think except I know that business is being conducted at this early hour there. Fishermen come in. Ships sail out of the harbor. Local merchants buy goods. Maybe Ivan is right in the thick of it."

The hair on the back of Gray's neck began to

stand up. Once again, it felt like he was missing something. Something crucial. Significant. The connection was right there, but it was like he couldn't make it.

"None of this makes sense," Luke said carefully as he eyed the others. "Ivan traffics women to Mexico, selling them after herding them onstage to a group of buyers. We know he has various seedy businesses he works with. His flight history is chock full of trips south. Why the fuck is he in Baltimore?"

"It's the harbor," Gray said, realization suddenly dawning on him. "He said he'd send her offshore. He could be dumping her body or—" He cut off, the thought too much to bear.

"Selling her." Luke's voice was low and deadly. "Moving her onboard a ship. He can pack women in like chattel and send them off to buyers overseas. He's either putting them on a private vessel or potentially using one of those big container ships."

Jett rose from the table, his eyes hard. He pointed at West from across the conference room. "Get into those camera feeds. We need eyes on the scene right now. Every damn terminal in the harbor. Find out what ships are sailing this morning out of Baltimore. We need destinations. Manifests. Let's figure out which ship he could be putting women on."

West grabbed the secure line, calling his team of IT gurus. He was already barking out orders before Gray could process what was happening.

She'd be gone. Untraceable. And possibly in the hands of men even worse than Ivan.

Gray jumped up from the table so fast he knocked his chair over. "We have to get to Baltimore. It's almost dawn." His gaze swept over his teammates, landing on his boss. "I'm calling Boone. He lives in DC and can get there quickly."

Jett nodded his approval. "Bring him in. I've got some old buddies stationed at Joint Base Andrews that could meet us there as well. I'll arrange for a helo to transport the team. Pack up your gear."

"It's well over an hour flight time. Boone will get there before us," Gray said.

Jett hadn't brought on anyone new yet because the team functioned so seamlessly together. A new man could throw things off balance—or shift things in their favor.

Jett's eyes met his. "Then he'll have a head start."

Twenty minutes later, the men were climbing onboard a helo. Jett had a helicopter pilot at the ready in his vast arsenal of contacts. While the men typically flew commercial flights, they did what they had to do when shit hit the fan. Boarding a private helo wasn't exactly out of the norm. It wasn't a military aircraft, but it would get them there quickly just the same.

Gray adjusted his Kevlar vest, wincing slightly. Hell if his scars didn't feel tight and itchy right now. Stress sometimes made his nerve endings flare up, his entire body feeling over-sensitized. Prickly. He'd do anything to get to Lena though. Bear any burden. This was nothing compared to the hell she was living.

He swiped the screen and lifted his phone to his ear. "You still in DC?" he asked as Boone answered.

The crack of the cue ball sounded in the background, and Gray heard low conversations and music playing. The sound of drinks being poured. "Roger that. Is something wrong? You don't usually call me at three a.m."

Gray didn't even ask why his buddy was out at this

hour. "Lena was kidnapped. We've traced her to Baltimore's Inner Harbor."

"Whoa," Boone said, the noise getting quieter. Gray heard a door open, and then Boone must've stepped outside into the night. "She's the woman you mentioned before? And of course I remember that, because you never mention anyone."

"It's her," Gray confirmed. "She was kidnapped by the head of a large sex-trafficking ring. We have a location and are staging a rescue op. There are multiple men involved, her kidnapping part of a massive operation. I need a favor."

"Anything."

"We need another sniper."

Chapter 20

The vehicle came to an abrupt stop, Lena nearly falling forward and smacking her head on the seat in front of her. They'd gagged her again after she screamed, two big men sitting on either side of her as they rode toward a loading area of a huge terminal. A massive crane was lifting another container onto the ship, but there weren't any other workers in the area they'd parked. It was secluded. Hidden. And she whimpered in fear as they pulled forward again and she saw a huge metal container forty yards away.

The final cargo was being loaded right now, and she was about to be locked away in a metal box and lifted onto a ship. Gray would never find her.

One of the men sprayed a marking on the side of the container with a can of spray paint, and she wanted to vomit. They were tagging it. Marking her location. She was being sent God knows where, and someone evil on the other end of the line would have her in their clutches.

Noise from the shipyard could be heard around them, but there was no one to see these men herding her into the steel container.

Ivan had long since disappeared, leaving his men to do his bidding. Tears streamed down her cheeks as her frantic gaze scanned the area. She saw other maintenance trucks coming and going from a distance, but no one noticed her. It was too dark, and they were too far away.

Tearfully, she spotted a security camera on the door of a small building. Sniffling, Lena looked right at it, almost willing someone to find her. Help her. Save her from this hell.

"Let's move," one of the men said. She stumbled, and he hefted her over his shoulder, laughing. Her dress was dirty and torn, her hair a mess, and she had scratches on her skin from stumbling around earlier. Now she was dangling over this guy's shoulder like a sack of potatoes. "Pity the boss didn't want to let us give you a proper goodbye," the man said, smacking her ass and then squeezing it. Lena's stomach roiled, and then he was walking right into the dark metal container, moving through a maze of boxes.

Another man held a flashlight, guiding their way, and she began to think she might vomit right into her gag.

The guy carrying her unceremoniously dumped her on the hard metal floor, lifting her arms forward. He secured handcuffs around her wrists, right over the zip ties, and locked her to a heavy metal chain in the back. She was locked in place before she could move, shock setting in. They'd done this before. Shipped people. Sold women.

The guy with the flashlight sneered. "You would've done good on the auction block. Plenty of men would've paid for night after night with a woman like you. Guess the boss got an offer he couldn't refuse."

The men turned, walking away, and leaving her there without so much as a backward glance. "We should hit up the hotel in Tijuana for our next assignment. I could use some fresh pussy. If you work extra shifts down there, sometimes you get to sample the goods for free."

"Fuck yeah," the other guy chuckled, their voices getting quieter. "I wouldn't mind seeing how many bitches I could tap in one night."

The light disappeared along with her captors, leaving her in the dark. A metal door slammed shut, the final nail in her coffin. Lena tried to shift positions, but she could barely move. She was literally shackled against the metal wall, cold, scared, and helpless. And the worst of it all? Gray would never find her. Never. She'd rather die than be a sex slave to some monster, but she had absolutely no choice in the matter.

***

The rotors of the helicopter nearly drowned out everything else, the thump, thump, thump matching the beating of Gray's heart. It was taking too long. They were too far away. He clicked the mic on his headset. "ETA?"

"We're twenty minutes out," the pilot said. "We'll be landing at oh-four-thirty."

Jett's voice came over his headphones. "The

Baltimore PD contacted the harbor master and Coast Guard. No ships are sailing until we arrive."

"Thank God," Gray muttered.

His teammates around him shifted, growing more alert as Jett continued.

"It took more time than I'm happy about to get everything in place, but we're a go," Jett confirmed. "You'll land on a helo pad near the harbor. West informed me that security cameras spotted several men forcing a woman past some warehouses just over an hour ago. She was spotted again at terminal four shortly after, looking directly at a security camera."

"It's Lena," Gray breathed, relief coursing through him. The men forcing her to walk with them meant she was alive. Resisting. His girl was a fighter, and he was counting on her to stay safe until he got to her.

"What's the plan, boss?" Luke asked.

"A crane at terminal four was loading a massive container ship setting sail to China. The crew is eager to leave and unhappy with the delay. West is trying to gain access to all security cameras in the vicinity to determine exactly where Lena was stashed."

Gray clicked his mic, eyeing his teammates. "They must've loaded her into a metal shipping container."

Ford nodded, his gaze a mixture of sympathy and anger. None of the men would want their women to go through anything like this, and Lena? She was part of the team. Gray's girl. His buddies might've given him shit for making out with her in the armory, but damn. She was it for him, and they fucking knew it.

"We'll get her," Sam said, his eyes hard. "We're not leaving the harbor without Lena. Boone should already be in place by now. As soon as the helo lands, we'll be a go."

"Boss, what happened to the men from Andrews?" Luke asked.

"On their way to provide backup," Jett confirmed. "They'll help secure the area but are active duty. They won't engage unless lives are at stake."

"Lena's life is at stake!" Gray exclaimed.

"Understood. Their orders, however, are to provide security at the scene. They'll be working along with the Baltimore PD. Not much I can do about it unless they choose to disobey their commanding officer."

"I don't miss the military at all," Nick muttered.

Ten minutes later, the Inner Harbor came into focus in the distance, the lights from the city gleaming off the water. The earliest hints of sunrise were beginning, the dawn of a new day nearly making his breath catch. Lena had been missing since yesterday. Time felt meaningless during the long night, but she'd been gone since yesterday afternoon. He feared what condition they'd find her in and prayed she was okay and could hold on until he got to her.

The helo landed at a heliport, Jett having already smoothed the way for their arrival. As soon as the landing skids touched the ground, the men were hopping off, ducking low under the still-spinning rotor blades and moving forward.

"The container ship is on the west side," Luke said, pointing in the distance. "Shit. Look at all the police arriving. I hope if the tangos are still here, they don't panic and do something drastic."

Worry coursed through Gray. If Lena was indeed locked in a shipping container, what could they do to her now? Unless she wasn't alone yet and still had a thug guarding her. If Gray lost her when he was this close....

"Boone's in position," Jett said in a clipped tone over the headsets. "I have him in a sniper's nest above the loading zone. He'll have a view of the entire area. Nick can get in position on the opposite side. There are vehicles parked there. If Ivan or his men attempt to escape with Lena, Nick will take them out."

"Roger that," Nick said as he clicked his mic.

"Can Boone hear us?" Luke asked with a frown.

"Negative. Not over the headsets. He got here quickly and has been lying in wait," Gray said. "Jett had a hunch the cargo ship would be the likely extraction point, and the surveillance footage by the warehouse and terminal proves it. The ship is so large, nothing else is docked here, so it made sense to get him in position. Boone's got his cell if I need to reach him."

"Affirmative," Jett said. "I've been in contact with Boone since his arrival. I've sent him the surveillance footage we have, as well as descriptions of the men traveling with Lena."

Gray felt his pulse pounding, the night air washing over him. It was cold as hell with the breeze blowing off the water. He'd donned long sleeves, but that was mostly to disappear into the shadows. Ivan's men didn't know they were coming.

Suddenly, gunfire erupted from all around them, proving he'd been mistaken. Gray dove behind a parked vehicle, rolling on the concrete as his teammates also hit the ground. It almost felt like a goddamn ambush.

"Guess we've been spotted," Sam quipped.

"SITREP!" Jett barked.

"Shots fired," Luke said in a calm voice. Several more gunshots sounded, coming from multiple directions. "The Baltimore PD have engaged with two subjects. Two tangos taken out. Everyone okay?"

"Roger."

"Affirmative."

"Ready to roll. Don't suppose any of them were Ivan," Ford said.

"Nah. That'd be too damn easy," Nick countered. He pointed to an area in the distance atop a warehouse as the men all rose to their feet again. "I'll set up there. It covers the parking lot and is on the opposite side of where Boone's located. We'll have eyes on multiple areas."

Gray nodded, and then Nick was turning and jogging away, his rifle slung across his back. He spoke quietly into his headset, notifying Jett that he was getting into position.

"We're moving in," Gray said, beginning to jog toward the loading area. While the Baltimore PD had been made aware that a team of former soldiers was moving in to retrieve a hostage, he wasn't sure they knew what to make of it. Normally, the FBI would be involved in something like this. Gray wasn't even sure that Jett had notified his contacts at the Bureau. Everything about this mission was unconventional, from operating on U.S. soil to saving the woman he loved. And yes, he loved Lena without a shred of doubt in his mind. He'd been falling slowly for her ever since they met, and now it felt inevitable that she was the one. He just had to get to her in time.

His gaze scanned the area, taking in the massive crane and multiple stacks of containers aboard the vessel. He looked over the rows and rows of various colored metal boxes, all of them looking ominous in the dim morning light. It felt like Lena was inside a casket—alone and cold, no doubt in the dark, and probably without food or water. He swallowed down his fear, taking a shaky breath. They'd search them all if they had to. Failure wasn't an option.

A loud fog horn sounded, indicating a ship's eminent departure. Gray nearly stumbled, watching in shock as the massive container ship began to slowly move away from the dock. A tugboat operator began yelling from the shore, waving his hands frantically. "Someone stole my tug! Stop! Stop them!"

A police officer and harbor security ran by, walkies in hand. "Alert the Coast Guard! Repeat. Alert the Coast Guard! There's an unauthorized departure of the Container Ship Apollo from terminal four. They are not allowed to leave this area. Over."

"No!" Gray yelled, sprinting toward the massive ship. He didn't even care if he was in danger from whoever had fired at them before; he couldn't let the ship sail without him.

Gray heard static over his headset and then Nick's voice. "I'm in position. There're two tangos approaching from the south. I've got them in my sights."

Jett's command was final. "Take them out."

Two gunshots sounded, the men crumpling to the ground behind him. Had Nick taken the kill shot or Boone? Gray couldn't tell from this angle. Maybe they'd each taken out a tango. Panic rose within him as the ship began to fire its engines. This was a massively crowded harbor. If someone had commandeered the vessel, it could be dangerous to everyone around them.

Helicopters began to circle in the air, searchlights pointing down at the ship. "This is the United States Coast Guard," a voice said over a megaphone. "Cease and desist all operations of Container Ship Apollo. You do not have permission to leave the harbor. Repeat. You are not authorized to set sail."

"We're going to be too late!" Ford shouted, running at Gray's side. Gray sprinted faster, leaping through the air and landing in the icy cold water. Shock washed over him from the chill as he plunged into the icy depths, and then he pushed upward with his arms, kicking hard and resurfacing. Gray swam to the bow of the ship, forcing his body to move in the cold. He heard Ford shouting behind him, and then Jett's voice over the headset. The ship continued to move slowly away from the pier, and Gray was already climbing the ladder, his hands like ice. He nearly slipped, almost falling back into the water, but held steady.

"There's someone else on the bow," Jett said into the headsets.

"Roger that. I'll be careful." Gray climbed the rest of the way up, shaking in the cold. His body couldn't lockdown now. It couldn't. Not after he'd endured so much. Briefly, his mind flashed back to the desert. The searing pain. The whippings. The sweltering tent. It felt like a thousand tiny knives were cutting into his skin right now, prickling every nerve ending, but he pushed on, flinging himself onto the bow.

The ship was still moving as the helicopters circled. Gray clicked his mic. "Do they know who I am?"

"Affirmative. They won't be shooting at you," Jett confirmed.

"Well thank God for something going right," Gray muttered. He spotted a man's big sweatshirt in an area where some gear and equipment was stored. The ship had departed so rapidly, someone had no doubt dropped it there in the rush. Gray heaved himself over and remained low, stripping off his Kevlar vest and soaked shirt. He slid the sweatshirt on, cringing at the feel of it against his scars, then strapped the wet vest atop it. His back was the last thing he needed to worry about right now. It was surprisingly easy to ignore given how cold the rest of his body was.

Gray checked his weapon, peering around the area, and rose to his feet.

The helicopters continued circling above, the sun rising further over the harbor. It would've been a nice sight, the sun gleaming off the sparkling water, except his girl was trapped somewhere on a runaway ship. Gray took several steps as he took in the massive vessel, hopelessness battling against anger within him. There were so damn many containers. Hundreds. It would take days and the entire team to thoroughly search each one. They could've stashed Lena anywhere. And how sick did those men have to be to put a woman inside, to sell her then ship her off like an object.

He clicked his mic. "Do we have any idea what type of container Lena was loaded in? Color, description, anything?"

"Negative," said Jett. "West is working on obtaining all the footage from terminal four's loading area."

"There's a goddamn crane right there," Sam said. "Didn't the operator see anything? If they were still loading containers onto the ship, Lena must be in one on top of the stack."

"Let's question him. He might've been paid hush money, but we'll get him to talk," Ford replied.

Suddenly, a gunshot rang out, and Gray dove to the ground. A second shot sounded, ricocheting off the metal. "I'm under fire!" he yelled. He lifted his rifle, aiming it up against an unknown enemy that was currently out of sight.

"I can see a man running toward the bow," Luke said from the pier. "White male. Dark pants, red shirt, black hair. He scaled the containers and is looking for you down below."

"I don't have a shot," Nick said, his voice strained. "Gray, I don't see you either."

"Fuck!" Gray swore, army crawling along the ship's surface as the man fired his weapon again. If Gray could get to the end of the row of shipping containers, he could get the guy in his sights and return fire. Right now, he felt like a sitting duck. "I hope like hell Boone can see him."

"Drop your weapon!" a voice from the police helicopter said over a megaphone, their floodlights turning toward the area.

"I still don't see him!" Gray yelled. "I don't have a visual!"

Suddenly, a single shot fired from the direction of the loading dock, coming from more than one hundred yards away. Gray heard a grunt and gurgle as the man fell to his death, landing far too close for comfort. The tango had practically been right above him.

"Boone took him out," Nick said calmly over the headsets.

"Thank God," Gray muttered, standing. Blood

was pooling by the head of the man who'd fallen, but Gray didn't have it in him to feel any remorse. No doubt this lowlife was one of Ivan's men. The ship was still moving toward the center of the harbor, commotion surrounding them onshore as more authorities were notified of the chaos.

"They're going to try to leave the harbor and sail away," Ford said, watching from the dock. "It looks like they're attempting to turn the ship."

"It doesn't matter. I'm onboard and won't leave without Lena."

"We've got another problem," Luke said, his voice urgent over the headsets. "There's black smoke rising from the ship."

"What?"

"I don't know if it's a fire onboard or trouble with the engine, simply causing something to smoke. Either way, it doesn't look good."

"God damn it! I'm not leaving this ship without Lena!" Gray began walking down the row on the starboard side, looking up at the stacks of containers. The most recently loaded cargo was of course on top, but he still didn't know which one to begin searching. It would take hours to break into all of them—time he didn't have. Just scaling to the top was going to be a problem.

"Lena!" he shouted, his voice nearly drowned out by the helos. Damn it. Even if she was inside, he'd never hear her calling back to him.

Gray paused, carefully assessing each one. How did the Chinese buyers know which container held their merchandise? A dock worker in China had to be in on the scheme, unloading the women once they reached their destination. Was there a word or marking they'd look for? Some other indication to let them know their live cargo was inside?

"What's the status on the surveillance footage?" he asked urgently into his mic. "Do we know the container Lena was put in yet?"

"Negative," came Luke's worried reply.

Gray moved to the bow, scanning the top row there. This section of the ship seemed the most likely spot the container had been stacked given the ship's position at the dock. He could be wrong, but he had to start somewhere. Adrenaline pulsed through his veins, all his senses on high alert. Gray stood there assessing. Calculating. The sunlight warmed his face. He could smell the scent of fish and brine and water. Hear the sirens and helicopter rotors. Feel the chill from his wet pants, socks, and boots. See the rows and rows of cargo.

There. One of the containers had a marking on the side that looked like spray paint. Was it graffiti or something more?

"There's something written on the top blue container, left corner of the bow," he said, his hand on his mic.

"What's it say?" Ford asked.

"I can't make out the markings. Thirty something. Thirty-six? It might say thirty-six D."

"Thirty-six D? What the hell does that mean?" Luke asked.

Sam clicked on his mic. "Doesn't sound like any damn GPS coordinates. Maybe they're marking a woman's measurements on the side of the container. It's sick as hell, but what if it means there's human cargo inside? Those are somewhat innocuous letters and numbers unless you knew what to look for."

Gray breathed in, suddenly knowing Sam was right. It was all kinds of twisted, labeling the cargo like Lena was a fucking object, not a woman, but he was thankful this shipping container looked different than the rest. The alternative of Lena remaining trapped wasn't a thought he was going to entertain. Black smoke continued to billow in the sky. It wasn't getting worse, but it also wasn't getting better.

"I'm going up," Gray said, trying to figure out the best way to scale all the containers. His gaze landed on a coil of rope, no doubt undone from when the ship had been docked. How would he secure it to the top though? He didn't have repelling gear.

"The Coasties will give you a lift," Jett said over the headsets. Gray blinked in surprise as a helo came closer, hovering above him. The rotors blew cold air down over him, and his feet felt numb from being in wet socks and boots. His boxers and pants were frigid, and the irony that he might literally have blue balls wasn't lost on him. Gray hoped all his appendages were okay after that dip in the icy water. Saving Lena was worth it though, consequences be damned.

More sirens sounded as firetrucks began to arrive on scene, and the Apollo continued its hopeless turn, nearly getting stuck in the harbor.

"Who the hell is piloting that thing?" Sam asked over the headsets.

"Not the harbor master. He's on the dock with a tugboat driver," Luke said.

"Well fuck," Gray muttered. "Hope it's not our buddy Ivan."

He didn't have time to worry about Ivan now. A rope dropped from the helo, and Gray grabbed hold, knowing he wasn't wearing the right gear. Normally, they'd hook in with carabiners, securing themselves to the line. "Stand by," Jett ordered, his voice gruff.

"No! I'm ready to go up!" Gray yelled.

"And risk Lena when you retrieve her?" Jett asked over the headsets.

Gray muttered under his breath as the Coasties threw down a second line with two safety harnesses attached. No doubt Jett had quickly brought the Coast Guard up to speed.

Gray grabbed the harnesses, quickly stepping into the leg loops of one and securing it around his chest. While he wasn't worried about his own safety, if he rescued Lena, they'd need to be quickly extricated from the still-smoking ship. Gray tightened the harness, securing it to the line, and signaled. He clutched the second harness in his hand, and then he was rising to the top of the stacked containers. Another gun shot sounded, and he cursed, trying to duck as his heartbeat accelerated, the thumping pulsing in his ears. Maybe that sound was the helo. At any rate, Gray was dangling in the air like a fish caught on a line, the perfect target.

"Shots fired! Shots fired!" Gray yelled.

He could see his teammates running on the dock but didn't see the shooter.

"I've got him in my sights," a deep and deadly voice said over the headsets. "Taking the kill shot." A single shot rang out before Gray could process what he'd just heard. He looked around, noticing his teammates surrounding a person on the ground. "The tango is down," the sniper confirmed.

"Shit. Boone, is that really you?" Gray asked.

"Roger that, buddy. Your boys here finally brought

me a headset. That's the second mofo I've taken out for you today. Guess you owe me a couple of beers for that."

Gray laughed, despite the gravity of the situation. That was Boone for you. Calm as hell, a crack shot, and with a dry sense of humor that you never saw coming. "Sure thing, man. As soon as I get my girl."

"Roger that. And hurry the hell up. My ass is freezing out here."

The helo shifted, and Gray landed on the top of the blue shipping container. He felt like he was on top of the goddamn world. His girl was hopefully within his reach. His old buddy had literally saved his hide. And Gray was about to rescue the best thing that had ever happened to him.

Gray jogged to the edge of the container, studying the door on the side. He blinked in shock. There was nothing where the padlocks were supposed to be. Either they'd loaded it so fast onto the ship that they'd forgotten to secure the damn thing, or he was in the wrong place.

Gray swung over the side, still secured by the rope on the helo. He almost felt like a fireman conducting a technical rescue, hanging from a line as he breached a vehicle. Except the metal that held Lena seemed more like a coffin. Did she have enough air? Was she coherent? Was Gray even in the right place?

He flipped the tabs back where the padlocks were supposed to be, then turned the handles ninety degrees to open the huge door. Signaling, he unclipped his carabiner and swung inside, his feet thumping on the metal as he landed. Gray slid his flashlight free from his cargo pants, turning it on and aiming it into the dark, cold space.

"Lena." His voice was low. Hoarse. He hardly dared to hope that she was actually here. The thump, thump, thump grew quieter as the helicopter hovered above, the metal from the cargo container slightly dulling the sound. Gray studied the boxes stacked in there for a moment, his mind flashing back to the armory and inventorying supplies at headquarters. "Lena!" he called out, trying to keep his hands from shaking as he aimed the light around the space. "Are you in here? It's Gray! Lena! Where are you?"

A whimper sounded from way in the back, and then Gray was shoving boxes aside, scrambling over them in his haste. "Lena!" he called again, shining his flashlight above him to light the way. His rifle was slung over his back, his Kevlar vest shielding him from any stray bullets to the chest, and his heart was thumping wildly.

More whimpers and sounds of pain made his chest clench.

"I'm coming!" He jumped over a box and jogged toward the back, his heart in his throat as his flashlight finally landed on a pale, trembling woman gagged and chained to the wall. He nearly did a double take as he realized it was Lena. She was ghostly white, in shock, wearing a pretty floral dress that wasn't at all appropriate for the winter morning. The baby shower. The abduction. The past twenty-four hours' worth of events played like a movie reel in his mind. And despite it all, she was still the prettiest damn thing he'd ever seen.

"Lena!" he yelled out again, rushing to her.

She shook, crying, seemingly not believing he was real.

"Shhhh. It's me, baby. You'll be okay now. I'm

here." He gently removed the gag from her mouth and collected her in his arms as she sobbed, her body far too weak and cold. She was chained to the back of the shipping container like a goddamned animal, but she managed to clutch onto him anyway, her head against his chest.

She was alive. Breathing. Clinging onto him like he was her lifeline.

Gray clicked his mic, wondering if his comms would even work from inside the cargo hold. "This is Gray. Repeat. This is Gray. Do you copy?"

Static crackled over his headset, and then he heard Jett's voice, relief washing over him. "Roger. What's your status?"

His eyes burned with tears as he held his trembling woman, and he blinked them away, his voice hoarse. "I found her. Repeat. I found her. Lena requires immediate medical attention. Fluids. Warm clothes. Meds. We need to get her medevac'd to the nearest hospital, ASAP. They've got her chained to the wall in this goddamn thing."

"Roger that," Jett said, his voice hard yet tinged with relief. "The Coast Guard helo is standing by, waiting for extraction. Once you're both inside it, they'll give you a lift straight to the closest hospital. I'm sending up the team."

"Tell the helo to send down a basket," Gray instructed. "I don't think she's strong enough to bring up on the rope."

He set down his flashlight, leaving it on, but didn't hear Jett's next words over the headset because all of his focus was now on the woman before him.

"Gray?" she asked. "Is it really you?"

He pulled back, searching her watery gaze. Her

cheek was red and bruised, like she'd been smacked, and he was almost too afraid to ask if she'd been hurt elsewhere. The chains that held her to the wall meant she'd barely been able to move while in the metal container. He couldn't imagine staying in the same position for days on end while the ship sailed around the world. His gaze had swept the ground as he'd rushed to her, and he'd seen no food. No water.

They deserved to die a slow death for leaving her like this.

"It's me, baby girl," Gray said, running a hand over her tangled hair. "It's really me."

"I thought I was dreaming. Hallucinating. They drugged me again, but you found me," she said, tears smarting her eyes. "You really found me. I tried so hard to be strong. I knew you'd come."

"Of course I would. I will always, always come for you," Gray said, his voice thick with emotion. "And I'm so sorry that I wasn't there yesterday," he added, his voice catching. "When we realized you were gone—" he cut off, choked up.

"They're the ones to blame for this, not you," Lena said vehemently. "They're animals. They've been stalking me all along like I was their prey."

"Are you hurt?" he asked, blinking away his own tears as he frantically assessed her, his big hands lightly running down her bare arms. "Damn. You're freezing," he murmured, rubbing her arms gently. Her feminine, pink dress was ripped and dirty, but she was clothed. Talking with him. Not screaming in pain. His gaze tracked down over her body, and he didn't see any blood or major injuries. The possibility of injuries he couldn't see chilled him to the bone. Had she been raped? Assaulted? He could hardly choke out the words.

"I'm not hurt. Not really. Just some bruises and scrapes. Ivan tied me up again and threatened me, but it was mostly just a big game to him. He was going to rape me, but then one of his men thought someone was coming and would find us. They drugged me again and brought me here. Where are we?" she asked. "A harbor, but where?"

"Baltimore's Inner Harbor."

"What happened to Ivan? After we got here, he left me with his men to be loaded on the ship."

"I'll explain later," Gray murmured. "Let's get you out of these chains first," he said, removing a set of lock-picking tools from his gear along with a K-Bar knife. "Are you sure that you're really okay?"

"I am now that you're here."

"Then let's get you home," he said, gently massaging her wrists before cutting free the zip ties. She was handcuffed as well, the metal rings attached to the chain on the wall. He'd have to pick the lock to remove her chain and handcuffs, but all that mattered was that she was okay.

Voices came from the front of the container, and then Gray's teammates were rushing back as well, helping him to free Lena. "Shit. Let's get you out of those," Sam said, quickly working to pick the lock on the handcuffs. Ford had an emergency reflective blanket to wrap her in as well as several bottles of water, and Luke carried the medic bag, seemingly surprised she was standing there in one piece.

"There we go," Sam said, releasing her wrists from the cuffs. He tossed them to the ground, the metal clinking on the floor.

Lena practically fell into Gray's arms now that she

was free from the wall, and then he was kissing her, holding her, loving her. "I thought I lost you," he whispered almost desperately, the feeling of her body against him pure heaven. "I should've gone with you yesterday to get the food. I shouldn't have let you go alone."

"He never would've given up," Lena said. She suddenly stiffened in his embrace. "Ivan's expecting the money he demanded. He'll come after me again. He's not going to let this go."

"He's dead," Ford said quietly.

"He's dead?" she asked Gray in disbelief. Ford handed him the reflective blanket, and Gray began wrapping it around her shoulders. It did little to stop her trembling.

Gray nodded. "Ivan Rogers is dead. Boone took him out."

"Who's Boone?

"Long story. I'll explain it all to you later. Let's get you out of here and onto the helo. We're catching a ride to the hospital." The other men began to move to the front of the shipping container, holding flashlights to help guide Gray and Lena's way.

"Wait!" she said, reaching out to grab hold of Gray's arms. "What's going to happen now?"

"We'll fly to the ER and get you checked out. Probably have a hell of a story to tell the Feds. I'm sure they'll keep you overnight at the hospital, but I'll stay with you," he said, searching her worried gaze. "You won't be alone."

"But what about us?"

He quirked his brow.

"You were protecting me. Now Ivan's gone. What's going to happen to us now?"

Gray's gaze softened, taking in the achingly beautiful woman before him. She'd been through hell, and he'd reassure her as much as she needed. "You're it for me, Lena. The one. I'm not giving you up just because you don't need my protection anymore. You saved me, too, from my own demons. I'm yours as long as you'll have me."

"I'm yours, too," she said tearfully. "I've always been yours."

Gray gently palmed her cheeks, and then he kissed her in front of his buddies, slow and deep, his heart thundering against hers. Gray didn't care if the entire world saw how he felt for this woman. She was his. "I love you," Gray told her, his voice rough.

"I love you, too, Gray. I love you so much."

He kissed her again then pulled back, in awe at the strength and love emanating from Lena. He was sure the same thing reflected back in his own eyes. "Then let's get you out of here. We have our entire lives ahead of us."

Epilogue

One month later

The party was in full swing by the time Gray and Lena arrived at noon, pink and blue decorations everywhere in Jett and Anna's large home. "At least I didn't have to help plan the food this time," Lena joked, squeezing Gray's hand.

"Don't ever joke about that day," he groaned. But he ducked and kissed her temple gently.

She smiled up at him, flushing, and Gray knew she was thinking of him kissing her the same way that morning. He'd made love to her slow and sweet in bed, listening to Lena's cries of pleasure beneath him. After she'd come once, he'd pulled out and turned her over, putting Lena on her hands and knees. Gray had taken her from behind, thrusting deeper and rubbing her swollen clit until she came for him again. After Gray's own release, he'd hovered over her body, his so much bigger than her own. While he'd remained inside her slick channel, his cock still throbbing, he'd kissed her temple tenderly.

She'd shuddered again, gasping for breath, and he'd been nearly overcome with his love for this woman.

They hadn't spent a night apart since her kidnapping, their time in the bedroom both sweet and passionate. Gray loved taking Lena in all sorts of positions, and as he'd known would happen, she always came alive at his touch.

She'd brought Gray back to life, too. He still had nightmares. Scars. The need to feel cool air blowing over his skin, reminding Gray of his freedom. But Lena was always there to soothe him, bring him back to reality, and kiss away any pain.

"But joking about it means I'm alive. Free. And apparently late to parties," she teased.

Gray's lips quirked. "It was a hell of a morning, baby girl."

Her eyes lit up, and he ducked down for a long kiss. "We don't have to stay for the baby shower," he said huskily.

Lena playfully swatted at his chest. "Of course we do. What would everyone think if we ran off the second we arrived?"

"My buddies all have women," Gray said, his voice gruff. "They'd understand."

Lena burst into laughter, looking at him in a way that made his chest fill with male pride.

"You made it!" Anna gushed, rushing over to them with a huge smile and throwing her arms around Lena. Anna was showing more every day now, her belly swelling under the clingy dress she wore. Jett appeared beside her holding baby Brody, and Gray almost did a double-take. It wasn't often that he saw

Jett holding his child. Then again, he saw the boss at headquarters and in the middle of ops. The gatherings at his large home had grown fewer now that he had his own family.

"We did," Lena agreed, hugging Anna back. "It looks beautiful here!"

"I hired a party planner," Anna said as she finally pulled away, looking around the room. "Clara didn't want to use the original decorations, saying it was bad luck."

Lena laughed. "Well, I don't blame her. The shower that never happened was probably something we'd all like to forget. Oh, but the food looks spectacular," she said. Gray followed Lena's gaze to the table covered with sandwich platters, tiny appetizers, fruit, and a massive display of blue and pink cupcakes.

"Girl dinner," Sam quipped as he walked over with Ava.

"It's lunchtime," she gently chastised him. "And I think the food looks delicious."

"So do you," he said with a wink. Gray bit back his laughter, watching Ava snuggle up against Sam.

Gray turned and pressed his lips to Lena's forehead, feeling more content than he had in years. Lena had been through hell, but over the past month he'd fallen even more in love with her, if that was possible. He knew without a doubt his life wouldn't be the same without her in it.

"Hey guys!" Luke called out, walking over with Wren. Soon the entire team was gathered around Gray and Lena, saying hello and welcoming Lena back.

"I'm so glad you're okay!" Clara told her, giving

Lena a hug. "We've missed you at work, but you deserve every second of the time you've had off to heal."

"Thank you. I'll be back in the office soon enough, so we'll be able to catch up then," Lena promised, adjusting the purse she had on her shoulder. She looked gorgeous in her new wrap dress and sexy heels. Gray had wanted to peel it right off her, but he knew they both needed an afternoon with their friends. It might be a baby shower, but it was also the first time Lena had seen everyone together since the incident.

"Oh, I'm counting on it!" Anna called out. "We need some major girl talk to catch up. It's not the same without you there. Plus, who else do I have to talk clothes with? I think Clara is bored to tears when I gush about designer things."

Clara laughed. "Not bored. We just have different tastes."

"I'm glad you both made it today," Jett said with a warm smile as he walked over, handing Brody to his wife. "You've been greatly missed around the office, Lena, but deserved every minute of your R&R."

"Is that what we're calling personal leave now?" she asked lightly.

"I'll call it whatever I want," Jett quipped, but his eyes twinkled with amusement. "I know I've said it before, but I'm grateful as hell that you're okay and that the team got to you in time." Jett's gaze grew intense as he looked between Gray and Lena. "You two are good for each other. I always thought you were somewhat alike, but you kept your distance until it was the right time."

"Since when are you so sappy, boss?" Gray asked,

crossing his arms as he looked at Jett in amusement.

"What do you mean? This conversation never happened," Jett said dryly, and Lena burst into laughter.

"Gray didn't want to talk shop while I was on leave," Lena said, growing more serious. "I've been wondering something though. Whatever happened with Ivan Rogers' operations in Mexico? I know he's dead, but what about the sex-trafficking ring?"

"It all began to crumble once his homes were raided and employees arrested. This particular enterprise of moving women aboard ships was a new venture for him. It seems he was expanding his business when his sex-trafficking sales came to an abrupt halt. With some of his players taken out of operation, unexpectedly caught up in the raid of his private homes, his trafficking scheme started to fall apart."

"Thank God," she breathed, and Gray slid his arm around her slender shoulders, pulling her close.

"Are you okay?" he asked quietly as Jett moved back to be with his wife.

"Yes. Just overwhelmed. We've been through a lot, yet here we are. Nothing about life is easy," Lena murmured.

"Except loving you," he said, his voice thick with emotion.

She looked up at him, tears filling her eyes.

"I love you, Lena," he told her. "I probably have since the first moment we met. I just couldn't get out of my own way to realize it back then. I thought I lost you forever last month. I'm not really a religious type of man, but I thank God I got to you in time. You're the one for me, baby girl."

Lena threw her arms around his shoulders, beaming at him through her tears. "I love you, too, Gray. So, so much." His hands slid to the back of her head as he stared into her eyes, and then he kissed her in the middle of the party, probably far too passionately given their friends were standing around watching, but he didn't care. Lena pressed close to him as they finally came up for air, and his cock twitched against his boxers at the feel of her curves against him. He'd never get enough of kissing her. Loving her. Feeling her body against his every night.

"I want to move in together," he said suddenly, looking into her dark eyes. "I want a life together. And when the time is right and I've actually bought a ring, I'm going to ask you to marry me."

"Yes. Of course I'll say yes," she said, beaming with joy and excitement.

Gray kissed her again, practically grinning from ear to ear, and then he was wiping away her tears of joy. Life was certainly hard sometimes, some moments brutal, but the moments of joy? Those were pure magic.

"Let's get this party started!" Jett called out, clapping his hands together to quiet the room a moment later. "I think the pregnant ladies are ready to eat, and my wife ordered enough food for a hundred people. We better get started if we have any hope of finishing it all."

There was a knock on the front door, and Anna flashed her husband a look, hurrying over to answer it. Gray stilled as he heard the same deep voice that had come over his headset a month ago. He hadn't seen Boone that day because he'd whisked Lena onto the helo, but his friend had been watching over them from the sniper's nest, ensuring they made it safely out.

"I dropped by to give something to Jett, but I'm not coming in."

"Just for a minute!" Anna pleaded.

Gray took Lena's hand, leading her over to see his old friend at the door. Brief introductions were made, and then his boss was at his side. Boone lingered out in the cold, his broad shoulders and bulk practically filling the doorframe.

"I heard this guy owes you a beer," Jett said, clapping Gray on the shoulder as he handed over a longneck. Gray held it up to his friend, raising his eyebrows in question.

Boone looked amused. "Another time, buddy. I can't stay." He eyed Jett, his look assessing. "Gray said you had a new job offer for me."

"Damn right I do. Send over your papers, and I'll have my office get your clearances in order." Gray's gaze narrowed as he saw Boone hand his boss something. It looked like a small key, but Jett pocketed it without comment. The party behind them had briefly quieted as the others came over to say hello, giving Boone their thanks for his assistance during their op in the Inner Harbor.

"Sure you can't stay for a beer?" Nick asked, his eyes sharp. Both snipers, the men shared a quiet calmness. They'd worked together last month, both in position yet hundreds of yards apart, keeping the team safe as they watched from high above.

"Not this time, but I'll definitely hit up my buddy Gray soon for the drinks he owes me."

Gray smirked at his old friend. "Just name the place."

Boone nodded, and his gaze landed on Jett, a beat passing. "I'll have the papers to you Monday."

There was a shadow as the former soldier turned, his boots scuffing in the dirt. There were no heavy footsteps as he walked away into the cold winter air. Boone was silent. Deadly. And back in the game.